Dominique Chenot

Nice to see, good to eat

Wellness recipes

MONDADORI

Some of the texts and images in this volume are taken from
The Taste of Well-Being (Electa 2005)

Photographs by Erwan Frotin and Manuela Vanni

Translation into English by Studio g.due, Milano

Special Edition

First edition: June 2012

www.librimondadori.it

Printed in July 2015
at Elcograf S.p.A., via Mondadori 15, Verona
Printed in Italy

Contents

In presenting the work of someone I greatly admire, I believe it is permitted to be partisan. My meeting with Dominique was love at first sight. Though I firmly believed in the virtues of celibacy, a week later I asked her to marry me.
Thirty-five years later, she continues to fill me with wonder and I consider myself a very lucky man.
This love may well have a great deal to do with her culinary abilities, to the delight of our children and friends. Dominique is extraordinary in the kitchen. She knows all about the raw materials and how to prepare them for the table. If my library is crammed with books on philosophy, hers is well stocked with books on cooking and dietetics and it is natural that she has taken control of the dietary alimentation section of our health center. Despite the number of foodstuffs rigorously excluded from the composition of the detox and biolight menus, she knows how to get the best out of the team in the kitchen in quest of flavor, cooking styles and products. I hope you will relish this book and benefit from it with your loved ones.

Henri Chenot

This book is not meant to present a diet, but a set of dietary rules to be followed day by day while savoring the pleasures of the table, cooking, receiving and enjoying food with others: all values fundamental to the quality of life. The aim is to combine pleasure and health, without entering into a spiral of frustration.
I dedicate this book to all those who have collaborated in its writing, my kitchen team, especially my chef Günther Pirhofer, a faithful collaborator. I wish to thank my husband, who has always encouraged me yet is also a valuable critic of our creations.
I hope this book will prove a practical and useful ally, enabling you to keep in shape for many long years.

Dominique Chenot

In Dominique Chenot's kitchen

food groups

Which food?

It is impossible to cook healthy, balanced food unless you first know what eating correctly means and the kinds of food available. This is why I have devoted a large section of this book to the different kinds of foodstuffs, beginning by distinguishing between the three main food groups essential to our organism: glucids, better known as carbohydrates, animal and vegetable proteins, fats or lipids.

The glucids: vital to health or nutritional disaster?

The answer is clear: they may well be either. In fact the glucids, more commonly known as carbohydrates or simply "sugars," are our organism's main source of energy and therefore absolutely essential. They may, however, be harmful for our health if eaten in excessive quantities and in the wrong forms. Hence the "demonization" of sugar and carbohydrates (bread, pasta, etc.) in public discussions about diets and nutrition. For this reason we need to have a close look at the glucids, to better understand just which and how much we need to eat to be fit.

Depending on their molecular structure, the glucids are subdivided into "simple" or "complex":

Monosaccharides: these are simple glucids made up of a single molecule of sugar. They are assimilated directly and very rapidly by the organism. The best-known are glucose, fructose and galactose;

Disaccharides: simple glucids, made up of two sugar molecules. Digestive enzymes have to split the disaccharides into monosaccharides to be tolerated by the intestine, as happens, for example, with the enzyme lactase, which is essential for the digestion of lactose. They are: saccharose (common sugar), lactose, maltose.

Polysaccharides: complex sugars made up of a chain of glucose molecules of various lengths. These are the starches we find in cereals, potatoes, legumes and as cellulose in some kinds of fruit and vegetables. They are digested by the intestine after being broken down into simple sugar in the form of glucose. Glycogen is one of this group of glucids: in form it is close to starch; our bodies store it as their principal reserve of sugar. It is released by our liver and muscles whenever our bodies need it, for example during intense physical effort or when playing sports.

The role of the glucids: LGI is best!

The final product of the digestion of glucids is glucose, the only energy molecule that our body cells can use. In addition this is the fuel that our bodies need to perform all the biochemical reactions essential to the proper functioning of our organs. In nutritional value the glucids differ greatly in the speed with which they are digested and their use. It should immediately be said that the different rates of absorption cause different responses on the part of the organism. For example, the starches contained mainly in carbohydrates such as cereals, bread, pasta, potatoes, etc. take our enzymes much longer to break down than simple sugars. A poor daily intake of glucids may force the organism to draw energy from other sources, for example from our fatty tissue, by converting its fats into sugars, or even to make its own glucose, by taking some of the amino acids from the proteins of the mass of muscle.

All this naturally has harmful effects on the renewal of the cells and the composition of the body. On the other hand, if our intake of glucids is excessive, our body weight will be increased. In fact the body has a limited ability to store glucids, and if not used they are converted into fatty acids and so increase the amount of fatty tissue.

The body needs to take in regular amounts of glucids to meet its energy demands and keep the concentration of glucose in the blood (glycemia) relatively constant. But the crucial factor is what is termed the Glycemic Index of each foodstuff. The glycemic index (GI) means the capacity of a food containing sugars to increase the level of glucose in the blood. In this respect a distinction is made between glucids with a high glycemic index (HGI) (including all simple sugars) and glucids with a low glycemic index (LGI) (see complex sugars).LGI foodstuffs allow a gradual and slower build-up of glycemia, so they ensure a stable supply of energy evenly distributed in time. HGI foods, by contrast, sharply boost the glycemia levels, causing the body to produce an excess of insulin which rapidly stabilizes the glucose level in the blood. This creates "insulin peaks," which cause not only added weight but also various disorders and fatigue due to irregular glycemia! This is because one or two hours after consuming simple sugars, the body feels the urge to boost the organism again by consuming more sugar after the sharp fall in glycemia, though it has only returned to the point of departure. The result is a vicious circle! All the same, in choosing foods we have to remember their GI can vary considerably and is affected by the way they are cooked, their preparation or their processing by the food industry. For example, there is a big difference between white rice and whole rice, because refining damages the fibers which are very active in reducing the GI. The same is true of fruit: the whole fruit, rich in fiber, has a lower GI than fruit that has been juiced, centrifuged or made into jelly (which also contains simple sugars). So always remember that, even if the calorie count for a refined food and the corresponding whole food is the same, the presence of fibers in the former makes it better for you because the glycemic index is lower.

What counts: quantity

So we can say that the presence of fiber is essential to ensure the right GI! Vegetables rich in fiber should make up 60 percent of every meal, while the remaining 40 percent should consist of proteins or carbohydrates.

To sum up: glucids that are absorbed slowly are essential, but you have to be very careful about their quantity and quality! In a balanced diet for a young person, say twenty-one years old, they should never exceed 90 grams net per day (see the chapter on nutritional equivalents), but the quantity should be reduced as you grow older. Besides, about one-fourth of the population is able to tolerate a much lower quantity of glucids: just 50 grams net. Above this threshold, these people tend to gain weight rapidly, because their body is not capable of assimilating the glucids.

About sugars...

Honey: good and wholesome

It is clear from what was said above that sugar, especially refined white sugar, should have no place in our nutrition. Instead we should favor glucids that are absorbed slowly. All the same, not everyone finds it easy to give up all sweet flavors and so it is natural to ask what substitutes we should choose. Honey is very good and wholesome nutritionally. Natural honey, in fact, is 20 percent water; the rest of it is made up of two sugars, fructose and glucose. Honey is slightly less rich in calories than sugar and contains certain digestive enzymes, minerals and trace elements important for health. Honey also contains essential and highly beneficial hormones found in the plants and flowers where the nectar was gathered. Its energy can be used immediately and is very effective in sustaining physical effort. But it is still a sugar, so be careful not to eat too much! The total recommended quantity is no more than two teaspoons per day.

Fructose: immediate energy

This is a sugar naturally present in fruit. It is sweeter than honey. The body is able to absorb fructose without using insulin and so without involving the pancreas. This means that taken in moderate quantities it is not unhealthy, but it is still a simple sugar and is assimilated rapidly.

Sweeteners: better avoided

Artificial sweeteners are chemically synthesized sugars with a high sweetening power. The commonest ones are: Saccharine: artificial sugar derived from coal tar. It contains no sugar and is 300 to 500 times sweeter than sugar. Aspartame: a combination of aspartic acid and phenylalanine. It is 180 times sweeter than sugar. Synthetic products can disturb the metabolic balance, so it is far better to use natural products such as honey or fructose..

Proteins: the body's building blocks

Trying to eliminate proteins from our diet would be like trying to build a house without bricks. Proteins, built up out of chains of separate amino acids, are essential to the growth, repair and renewal of all parts of our organism. They form part of the cell structure of our skin, tissues, organs, muscles... and they also play a part in producing numerous hormones (for example insulin) and antibodies (of great importance to the immune system). Remember that some amino acids cannot be synthesized by the body (essential amino acids) and they have to be absorbed from our diet.

But again quantity is all important. The daily requirement of an adult is around 45-50 grams net, the equivalent of a steak weighing 125 grams (see the chapter on nutritional equivalents). For children, adolescents and women in pregnancy the quantities may be greater, since their bodies are growing or building, but they should never exceed 2 grams for every kilo of body weight. In short, it is useless to consume excessive quantities of protein as our bodies are unable to make use of it. In fact the opposite is the case. Surplus protein is converted into glucose by the liver and into waste products such as urea or uric acid, so placing a strain on emunctory organs like the kidneys and liver.

And not just animal protein...

We should be careful, however, to choose the sources of amino acids so as not to harm our bodies. In fact, the proteins found in red meat, especially, are often accompanied by excessive amounts of mainly saturated fats which slow down the digestion. An excess of animal protein is particularly dangerous: it produces intestinal putrefaction with the production of gas (such as methanol) that is cadaverine and putrescent, poisoning the organism and preparing the way for serious disorders. This means we should eat more vegetable proteins and limit our intake of animal protein, so reducing the production of various kinds of harmful waste. In addition, it is a good idea, when planning a meal, to accompany animal proteins with fruit and/or vegetables with outstanding antioxidant properties. Fish is a significant exception: fish proteins have a very high organic value. Moreover fish contains important Omega 3 polyunsaturated fats (above all found in fatty fish, mainly from cold seas). These fats have a protective action at the cardiovascular level and on the cerebral functions.
Proteins can be divided into two types:

Animal proteins	*Vegetable proteins*
found in:	found in:
Fish	Legumes
Meat	Soybean and derivates
Eggs	Cereals, but in smaller quantities
Milk and dairy products	

Vegetable proteins: legumes

(Soybean / Beans / Chickpeas / Lentils / Dried fava beans / Dried peas)
Legumes are rich in vegetable proteins: they contain percentages of up to 20-22 percent, the same quantity of proteins in a slice of veal. They are made up of: cellulose, fibers, vitamins, mineral salts and vegetable proteins that, though present in large quantities, are different from those found in meat. They are described as incomplete, since they lack certain amino acids. For this reason they have to be supplemented, for example with the cereals. A combination of legumes and cereals is excellent and contains the full range of amino acids. The advantage of vegetable proteins is that they do not contain cholesterol and saturated fats and this means they are highly suitable as supplements in a healthy diet. However, we have to be careful how we prepare and cook legumes. Being rich in cellulose and fiber, they may create problems if you tend to suffer from colitis, because they can cause swellings or abdominal pain. This is particularly true of thick-skinned legumes, such as chickpeas, which are more difficult to digest than thin-skinned ones such as lentils. For this reason it is a good idea to strain them after cooking. Then legumes often appear in complicated recipes, rich in juices or cooked fats, and this makes them even more indigestible.

Preparation and cooking of legumes

If dried, leave the legumes in water for several hours (about 6-12), so as to shorten the cooking time and so protect the minerals and vitamins, at the same time reducing the risk of swellings and flatulence.

Steam, boil or pressure cook them.

Never add baking soda (bicarbonate) to the cooking water! This destroys some B group vitamins and vitamin C! On the other hand, it is a good idea to add a piece of seaweed, which makes legumes easier to digest..

Soybean and its derivates

The proteins contained in soybean are the only vegetable proteins that are complete, meaning they contain all the essential amino acids. For this reason it is a good meat substitute. Soybean also contains calcium, magnesium, iron, vitamin E, folic acid and high quality fats.

Soybean: a legume rich in vegetable proteins, vitamins and minerals, and entirely lacking in gluten! It contains 18 percent more oil rich in polyunsaturated fatty acids than the other legumes and enhances the functioning of the liver. It is also used as a meat substitute as tofu, soybean noodles and in many other forms.

Tofu: curd made from the liquid extracted from the soybean. It contains 2 or 3 times more iron than a helping of cooked meat. It is low in calories (only 87 calories per 100 g), rich in fiber (3.5 g per 100 g), "good" fatty acids and lecithin. Being free from cholesterol, it is highly recommended for people suffering from cardiovascular disorders. It can be used in endless different ways: in meatballs, forcemeat, sauces, cakes, whipped or diced, sliced, breaded, grilled...

Soybean oil: this is a light oil, yellow and dense, extracted from the soybean. It is rich in fatty acids that enable it to control the cholesterol in the bloodstream. All the same, there are other oils that are better in nutritional terms.

Soybean stew: vegetable "meatballs" made out of soybean flour and water, then dehydrated. It is important to leave them in water for 20-30 minutes to cook them like a true meat stew.

Soybean flour: the flour made from the soybean lacks gluten and contains 2 to 3 times more proteins than wheat flour.

Soybean noodles (and other shapes): white transparent noodles made from soybean flour. Boil in water briefly (3-4 minutes) and serve with a sauce to taste.

Soybean milk: a white liquid extracted from the soybean.

It is called milk because it is an excellent milk substitute in a vegetarian or low-fat diet. There are also soy-based yogurts and desserts. It is a refreshing drink and contains all the isoflavons of the soybean, which are also important to maintain a good hormone balance in women.

Miso: a brownish paste made from soybean, and fermented wheat and/or rice. It is used to make an excellent vegetable stock, light and nutritious, for soups, risottos and minestrone.

It is an excellent substitute for bouillon cubes.

Soy sauce: a savory liquid condiment, used to flavor dishes of vegetables, cereals or legumes, making them easier to digest. Also known as Shoyu.

Tamari: soy sauce whose ingredients include fermented wheat or barley.

The lipids: the good and the bad

It should first be said that a completely fat-free diet is out of the question, in spite of dietary fads, because the lipids are an essential foodstuff. Their role is to supply the cells with energy in concentrated form (1 g of fat has a count of 9 Kcal), to bring essential fatty acids (which our bodies are unable to synthesize by themselves but have to take in with our food), and to assist in the assimilation of certain vitamins, called liposoluble vitamins, which can only be absorbed in the presence of fat. These are vitamins A, E, D and K. It is above all the excess of fats in our diet that makes us put on weight, because they end up being stored in the fat cells. Above all, remember that when they mainly take the form of animal fat, the excess produces serious heart disease. Besides, the more fat we add to our diet, the more our body produces galanin, a substance that in its turn increases our craving for fat! We need to know about the different kinds of fat and where they are found, how to use them and which to consume to derive their benefits without undesirable side effects. Warning: lipids are present in numerous foods in the form of added fats, such as oil, lard, butter, margarine, etc., widely used in the kitchen, because they are attractively flavored and make cooked food soft and tasty. To a great extent they are also found in our diet in the form of "invisible fats," like those in fresh meat and fancy meats (charcuterie), cheese, oily fruit, avocados, olives, etc., and in many processed foods, such as potato chips, mayonnaise, chocolate and all pastries.

Fats: be very sparing!

The quantity of fat in our daily diet should not be more than 20-25 percent of our calorie needs, preferably in the form of unsaturated fats or the fats in fish.
There are various types of fatty acids that have very different effects on our organism. We can examine them together.
Saturated fatty acids: these are essentially fats of animal origin (for example butyric acid, typically found in butter) and present above all in solid form. These fats are harmful as they damage the arteries. We find them in: butter, cheese, palm oil (highly saturated!), processed meats, fresh meat and numerous industrial products (cookies, pastries, etc.) You are advised to cut right down on saturated, added, transformed or "invisible" fats, and in any case they should never exceed one-third of the percentage of fat daily recommended. Better still, eliminate them completely.
Unsaturated fatty acids: these fats help prevent arteriosclerosis, so they can be recommended for people who have cholesterol problems. These oils, besides fighting harmful cholesterol (LDL), help restore the optimal levels of "good" cholesterol (HDL). Their role is essential: they help in the construction of cell membranes, in the growth and development of body organs, and play an important part in the nervous system and reproductive functions. Unsaturated fats are further divided into:
• *Monounsaturated*: found in vegetable fats, for example olive oil, colza (rapeseed oil, long controversial for its method of extraction in the past, but today, with different treatment, one of the highest quality oils), peanut oils, as well as in hazelnuts, almonds, avocados, and olives. Almost always found in liquid form, as in the case of olive oil or oils from other fruits or seeds. If consumed in the right amounts and raw, they are very important and highly beneficial to the organism.
• *Polyunsaturated*: these are called "essential oils," as they cannot be produced by the body and have to be taken in with our diet. They are found in many vegetable oils (oils obtained

from colza, olives, sunflower seeds, pumpkinseeds, sesame seeds, avocados, walnuts, etc.) and in fatty fish, which are also rich in Omega 3 and Omega 6 (tuna, salmon, eels, sardines, etc.)
Trans fatty acids: these are fats synthesized industrially by hydrogenating liquid vegetable oils to make them solid. Many kinds of margarine, for example, are of this type. These fats are the most harmful and should be rigorously excluded from your diet. They are often found in processed foods, so check labels carefully before buying.

Omega 3 and Omega 6

These are essential fats. They control the total cholesterol level, since they regulate its metabolism, affect enzymatic hormonal activity, protect cell walls, produce prostaglandin, boost the immune defenses and are essential to growth.
The first of the Omega 3s is linolenic acid, whose main sources are: linseed (50 percent), walnut and soybean oils. The sources of the Omega 6s is linoleic acid, present in oily fruits and alga spirulin in large amounts. Large amounts of both are found in the oils of fatty fish, especially those that live in cold water, like salmon.

- Daily intake of Omega 6 (contained in walnut, olive, corn and soybean oils, and in oily fruits): from 8 to 12 grams = 1 dessertspoon of walnut or sunflower oil. Larger doses may encourage the production of free radicals.
- Daily intake of Omega 3 (contained in linseed, walnut, colza and soybean oils and in fatty fish like salmon, tuna or sardines): these are useful in small quantities, from 1.5 to 3 grams per day, corresponding to 1 portion of 100-150 g of fatty fish or 2 dessertspoons of walnut oil.

But it all depends on the cooking...

Unsaturated fats have a drawback: they deteriorate during cooking, which causes them to release some highly toxic substances. So avoid heating these oils, above all sunflower and corn oils. If you have to, then use peanut oil for cooking, as its structure stands up to it better. In general, however, it is better to use nothing but raw oil, choosing those with a high proportion of polyunsaturated fatty acids and adding them to the cooked food as a pure condiment. Be careful not to cook fish long either. Polyunsaturated fatty acids deteriorate badly during cooking, losing part of their beneficial qualities.

Nutritional equivalents

Nutritional equivalents provide comparisons between different foods, showing the proteins, lipids, glucids, alcohol and calories they contain. They are very useful in making sure our daily diet consists of the right foods in the right quantities.

Protein equivalents

Daily net need of proteins: 40-50 g

- 200 g filleted beef = 41 g proteins =
- 250 g chicken breast
- 150 g prosciutto crudo trimmed of its visible fat
- 200 g fish
- 180 g dried legumes
- 120 g dried soybeans

Glucid equivalents

- 80 g wheat pasta = 250 Kcal =
- 70 g rice
- 300 g potatoes
- 70 g dried legumes
- 70 g bread
- 80-90 g wholemeal bread

Fat equivalents

- 10 g of oil = 9.9 g of fat =
- 15 g butter
- 15 g cream
- 35 g parmesan cheese
- 250 g natural whole milk yogurt
- 990 g natural skimmed milk yogurt

Alcohol equivalents

A topic that is often explored in our wellness centers is alcohol. Alcohol, like all stimulants, is in itself toxic, but it should be considered that a good glass of red wine of excellent quality, at lunch or supper, is strongly recommended as it contains antioxidants. For this reason it is above all recommended with meat, whose digestion releases several toxins into the intestine.

- 1 glass of red wine (about 150 ml) = 115 Kcal =
- 1 glass of white wine (about 150 ml)
- 2 glasses of beer (about 300 ml)
- 1 glass of sparkling wine (about 125 ml)
- 1 glass of whisky (about 75 ml)
- 1 glass of grappa (about 75 ml).

True or false?
The most frequent doubts about nutrients

1. Pineapple is slimming.
2. Fructose (fruit sugar) is a simple sugar like saccharose (white sugar) and has the same properties.
3. Which is the most dangerous?:
• fat accumulated on the upper part of the body.
• abdominal fat.
• fat on buttocks and thighs.
4. Fish contains fewer proteins than meat.
5. The fattest fish is leaner than the leanest meat.
6. Legumes are poor in nutriments.
7. Some oils contain more fat than others.
8. Margarine contains less fat than butter.
9. In a slimming diet you can eat all the fruit you like.
10. Demerara sugar has a lower calorie count than white sugar.

Answers
1. False. It is true that pineapple contains enzymes with lipolytic and proteolytic properties that can break down proteins and have a diuretic effect. But these enzymes are found in the core of the pineapple, which is normally discarded. Being a fruit, pineapple contains sugars, so it is not slimming!
2. False. It is a simple sugar normally present in fruit but much sweeter than honey. Fructose is absorbed slowly in the intestine without using insulin.
3. The most dangerous is abdominal fat because it can create cardiovascular disorders and is closely correlated with diabetes.
4. False. The protein content is identical.
5. True. The important difference is the quality of the fat in fish, which is polyunsaturated (Omega 3).
6. False. They are very rich in proteins and slow glucids and extremely rich in fiber.
7. False. All oils contain 9 Kcal per gram, but they should be chosen for their other qualities (oils obtained from the first pressing and cold pressed, organic oils).
8. False. It is still a fat. Choose margarines free from hydrogenated fats.
9. False. Remember that fruit, which contains sugar (4 Kcal per gram), should be eaten in moderation.
10. False. But raw sugar retains many mineral salts and fibers and has not been treated with chemicals during refining.

the essentials

Water: source of life and health

We can do without food for several days, consuming our body's stores, but we cannot last long without water, because we have no reserves of water and every day we eliminate large amounts of it: about 1300 cc through the kidneys, about 100 cc through the intestine, about 300 cc through respiration and about 300 cc through the skin, for a total of about two liters. Water makes up more than 60 percent of the human body. However, to make good the water we lose there is no need to drink two liters of water daily, as our food also contains a large amount: vegetables and fresh fruit are about 90 percent water, bread about 35 percent, lean meat about 76.6 percent, milk 87.3 percent, etc. The water we drink (usually one liter a day) and take in with our food is called exogenous, meaning it comes from outside us. Then there is another supply of water that is obtained when the proteins, fats, and glucids are burnt by our organism: this is known as endogenous water, meaning that its source is inside us. It makes a difference whether we drink before, during or after meals. To improve digestion we have to create a favorable environment: drinking during meals dilutes our gastric juices and weakens their digestive power. It is advisable to drink between meals on an empty stomach, so as to boost the moisturizing power of water. We should also drink water in the morning before breakfast and before going to bed at night.

Cereals: clean fuel

Cereals have always played an essential part in the human diet, from the beginnings of agriculture. Their importance in the history of the world is bound up with the growth of civilizations based on the discovery of how to cultivate cereals. Each continent has its own cereal crops: rice in the Far East, rye and barley in North-East Europe, wheat in the Mediterranean area... Cereals contain large amounts of carbohydrates and fiber, very limited quantities of fat and some essential amino acids, though in small amounts.
We can divide the cereals (and foods similar to cereals) into two groups (see table on p. 26).

Cereals: an important source of complex sugars

All the cereals described above and their derivates contain complex sugars which the body transforms into simple sugars. After being digested in the small intestine, they are absorbed into the bloodstream and supply the fuel needed by the cells and our metabolism. But we have to be careful not to eat too much! If the body has no need to use the sugars, it will immediately store them in the liver and muscles, where the body can draw on them rapidly for its needs during physical or mental effort. Cereals are therefore an excellent source of glucids, vitamins (E, B1, B2) and proteins, though they lack some essential amino acids.

Bread

Normally made from wheat flour. Cooking eliminates vitamin E and the gluten forms a soft, gluey substance that adheres to the walls of the intestine and slows the passage of other foods, causing intestinal fermentation and preventing the absorption of B group

vitamins. White bread is an entirely "devitalized" food since it lacks the vitamins and minerals embedded in the outer layer of the seeds. However wholemeal bread, and better still sourdough (naturally leavened) bread, contains all the nutrients found in the whole grain: vitamins, mineral salts, unsaturated fatty acids...
An increasing number of people are allergic to gluten; it can cause symptoms such as abdominal disorders and swelling, problems in the respiratory tracts and skin problems... However, products that contain gluten are easily replaced by equivalent foodstuffs: rice, crackers or noodles made from rice, corn (maize) and derivatives, millet, quinoa, tapioca, amaranth and pure buckwheat.

Fiber

This is the fibrous material that supports and holds together vegetables (fruit, vegetables, legumes, cereals).
Our bodies are unable to break down fiber, so this substance has a zero calorie count. It absorbs water, increasing its volume and forming a sort of net that helps eliminate the residues of digestion (including surplus fats and sugars). Foods rich in fiber satisfy our appetite quickly, as they require lengthy chewing, abundant salivation and the secretion of more gastric juices. By eating more fruit, vegetables and whole foods instead of high-calorie foods we can curb excessive appetite and follow a balanced diet better suited to our needs.

Potatoes

Potatoes are a source of carbohydrates and they remineralize and alkalize the body. They are 80 percent water. 100 g of potatoes supply 1.3 grams of fiber, 2 grams of proteins and only 75 Kcal.
Their very high protein content gives them a good draining power. Rich in phosphorus and B group vitamins, potatoes were long believed to be fattening: this is not true, provided they are steamed, boiled or baked complete with their skin and without added fats.
• 100 g of boiled potatoes contain 71 Kcal
• 100 g of baked potatoes contain 148 Kcal
• 100 g of fried potatoes contain 188 Kcal
• 100 g of potato chips (fried and packaged) contain 537 Kcal.

Food intolerance: gluten, lactose...

First of all we need to understand that an intolerance is not an allergy. Allergies trigger an immediate reaction (sneezing, eyes watering, skin rashes, etc.).
In the case of an intolerance, the reaction is much slower and the symptoms, varied and complex, may appear long after the food is eaten. They include fatigue, swellings, sleep disorders, headaches, bloating, rashes, abdominal pains, weight gain. What is the cause of food intolerances? Our body is unable to digest certain foodstuffs that cause intolerance, because it lacks the enzymes necessary to transform macromolecules into micromolecules. The macromolecules are not broken down and so remain permanently present in the organism, causing an immune reaction which raises the level of specific antibodies. Some aggravating factors, such as the intake of antibiotics or a consumption of large amounts of simple sugars and products made from white flour, also have the effect of making the intestine more permeable.
The result is that the macromolecules are not digested but pass into the body through the weakened intestinal mucosa, so giving rise to immune reactions and causing inflammation. The foods most often identified as the source of intolerance are currently the gluten present in cereals and the lactose found in dairy products and eggs.
Lactose intolerance is caused by our inability to digest milk sugars. This is an increasingly widespread disorder that results in symptoms such as flatulence, bloating, diarrhea, intestinal cramps, fatigue, skin problems, etc. Intolerance can greatly complicate cooking methods, but this book also takes this problem into account and provides recipes and hints which will benefit people suffering from food intolerance.

Fruit: essential every day

Fruit has been eaten since prehistory and cultivated for six thousand years. Every variety of fruit contains its own specific nutrients plus some shared qualities (being rich in water, vitamins, potassium, calcium, iron and magnesium; but also zinc, copper, sulfur). Fruit contains few calories and may be diuretic.

• Starchy fruits	rich in starches and sugars (chestnuts and dried fruit)
• Sugary fruits	rich in sugars (pineapples, figs, persimmons, grapes and dates)
• Acid fruits	rich in organic acids (oranges, mandarins, lemons, strawberries, raspberries, apples, pears, peaches, apricots, and grapefruits)
• Oily fruits	rich in fats (walnuts, hazelnuts, peanuts, almonds, pistachio nuts)

Fruit is indispensable in our daily diet. It is rich in vitamins, minerals and fibers, while its organic acids (citric acid, tartaric acid...) are completely oxidized by the human body to form alkaline compounds. So fruit helps alkalinize our organism. It resists the formation of acids and toxic substances from meat and fat, which are produced continually by the functioning of the body's cells and tissues.
When fruit is eaten on its own it remains in the stomach for a very short time. But if eaten

at the end of a meal rich in starches or proteins it will have to "wait its turn" to be digested, so causing fermentation. For this reason it is better to eat fruit on an empty stomach (at breakfast, before meals or as a snack).
There are exceptions: apples contain various enzymes that favor the digestion of starches by locking onto them. Pineapple and papaya also favor the digestion of proteins.

Vegetables: fiber and health

Vegetables are rich in water, vitamins and mineral salts.
They contain few glucids, proteins and lipids, have a very low nutritional value, but are rich in fibers. They have an alkalinizing effect in the stomach. Then there are vegetables rich in glucids (starches and sugars). Potato starch is easily digested and rapidly assimilated, which means it is not suitable for diabetics.
When vegetables are cooked they lose vitamins and mineral salts.

• Vegetables free from starch:	endives, lettuce, spinach,cabbage, green beans, cauliflower, broccoli, zucchini, eggplant, asparagus and mushrooms.
• Vegetables low in starch:	artichokes, carrots, parsley, radishes, celery, pumpkin.
• Vegetables with high starch content:	beets, brussel sprouts, onions, potatoes, leeks, turnips.

Seaweeds: a precious source of minerals

Seaweeds are plants that live in the sea. Different types exist, but all are rich in mineral salts (calcium, iron, zinc and iodine), vegetable proteins, vitamins (especially vitamin B and beta carotene), and fibers. Seaweeds are also used to produce the thickening emulsions and gels used in cooking (see: agar-agar). Seaweeds possess therapeutic properties, as in the treatment of arteriosclerosis, hypertension and bacterial infections. A piece of dried seaweed should therefore be added to all clear or vegetable soups: if you dislike the taste you can blend it so that the taste and consistency are lost among the other vegetables. The average nutritional content of seaweeds:
• 12 percent proteins
• 4 percent minerals
• fiber in significant quantities
Dried seaweeds should always be soaked before using. They can be served hot or cold; they can be boiled, grilled, steamed, sautéed or marinated in vinegar and tamari. Seaweeds (per 100 g) contain:
• calcium: 800-1400 mg (arame, wakame, kombu)
• iron: from 14 to 29 mg (arame, wakame, kombu)
• iodine: 190 mg (kombu); iodine is almost completely eliminated from cooking salt.

Dominique Chenot's hints

Eating and drinking for health

• Fruit not only has a detoxifying effect but is naturally rich in potassium, known for its diuretic properties. It supplies minerals that help strengthen the bones. Fruit is best consumed before meals: digestion is much faster if the fruit is eaten alone. If you eat it after a meal it will tend to stagnate in the stomach and being unable to follow the normal digestive path, will ferment, aided by the body's heat. It will soon make its presence felt...

• Beware of sugary drinks, including fruit juices. It is beneficial to consume the whole fruit because it will supply you with sugars, true, but also its abundant fiber. As for wine, you can certainly drink it but in moderation: preferably red, in combination with meat or fish rather than cereals. Remember that it turns into sugar. When eating cereals it is best to accompany them with water and lemon.

• Be careful not to eat too many raw vegetables, because they tend to cause swelling. Go for vegetable soups, which moisturize the body and furnish a good supply of vitamins.

• The organism functions all round the clock: 20 more calories each day add up to 1 kg more each year...

• Give a thought to seaweeds! They are rich in iodine (a thyroid-stimulating hormone) and thyroxine, they stimulate the metabolism, and provide the minerals we assimilate most easily. In short they are very beneficial (see p. 22).

• Why automatically take a tablet at the first onset of a headache or stomach ache? The body may be sending you a signal. Check what you have been eating, which is often the cause of these disorders.

• Breakfast is not optional. If you're going to use your car you fill up with gas first to avoid being stranded...

• Be careful not to eat too much in the evening. Choose lighter foods to encourage the secretion of melatonin during sleep. Whenever possible it is best to eat a light dinner and avoid going to bed soon after. For this reason it is also better to eat fairly early.

• Eating out is not the end of the world, quite the opposite! A tip on choosing from the menu: follow the same principles you would at home. Go for the same favorable combinations and avoid mixing carbohydrates and proteins.

• Hold the salt! Try using herbs or spices, fresh if possible, as a substitute. They will enhance the flavor and color of our dishes, limiting the need for salt. Don't put them in the blender or they will lose their natural qualities. Just chop them finely to get the most flavor out of them.

• Drink plenty of water! A very precious element, water eliminates waste with the urine. Your kidneys need a regular supply of water.
Remember the recommended amount is about 1.5 liters a day.
It may be useful to remember to drink a glass of water every time you lose it by going to the bathroom.

• If you don't like water neat, just add a little lemon or a small amount of cider vinegar so it is more effective in moisturizing the body. Drink teas made with herbs that favor lymphatic drainage or Sassy water (see recipe p. 139).

the daily diet

What and when to eat

"In the morning eat like a king, at noon like a prince, in the evening like a pauper." If you follow this popular maxim at table you will take the first step to healthy eating. We will now see in practice just what to eat and when in the course of the day.

Breakfast: the launch pad for our day
This meal influences our physical form all day long. A balanced breakfast supplies the ideal fuel for our cells. Vitamins, mineral salts and fruit fiber, complex glucids and unsaturated fatty acids from wholemeal cereals, proteins, etc. ensure our body gets enough energy. From the very start of the day it is important not to confuse counting calories with a healthy and balanced combination of individual foods. Here are various examples of the right kind of breakfast to do a morning's work without failing energies.

• Example 1
Fresh fruit (practically compulsory as a source of liquids, fibers, vitamins and sugars!), or centrifuged fruit or fruit juice; a slice of wholemeal bread made from buckwheat or emmer wheat, with an egg, soft-boiled or scrambled, with barley coffee or even better green tea with mint, sweetened with a little organic honey or fructose.

Dominique Chenot's hints

Combating stress
• Stress is one of the symptoms of a diet lacking in essential nutrients.
A shortage of magnesium leads to significant levels of fatigue, cramps or even sleep disorders. If your stamina is low, especially when the seasons are changing, you can make up for it by adopting a cure to boost your flagging energy.
• For example, why deny yourself a square of chocolate every day, as a moment of pleasure and an excellent barrier against stress? Dark chocolate is a great source of magnesium, which has a soothing effect. This trace mineral helps relax the muscles and nervous system.
A natural antidepressant, it releases endorphins, the pleasure hormones that promote a sense of wellbeing. As always, avoid excesses.
• Nuts of various kinds (walnuts, almonds, hazelnuts, etc.) are real safety valves against the adrenaline surges that the heart suffers as a result of stress. Rich in antioxidants, Omega 3, vitamin B6 and magnesium, nuts are an important ally against stress. The ideal quantity is 2 a day, to be inserted as desired in the menu.
• Some plants have an anti-stress effect that you can make the most of by drinking them as infusions. Hawthorn and passionflower have relaxing properties that promote relaxation and sleep, without any sedative effect. The habit of drinking some herbal tea after dinner will help your nights pass peacefully.

• Example 2
A probiotic product (such as "Bionessere") with a bowl of fresh fruit salad (made from fruit in season) with rolled oats, and green tea sweetened with fructose, rice malt or maple syrup.

• Example 3
Breakfast for sport-lovers:
an energy drink from tofu made by blending 50 g of soft or velvety tofu with a diced apple, a teaspoonful of sunflower or sesame or pumpkin seeds with 100 ml of rice milk, almond milk or oatmeal milk; a piece of fresh fruit in season; a cup of green tea before or after practicing sport.

Lunch: vegetables and carbohydrates are best

Remember that vegetable proteins follow a digestive path similar to that of carbohydrates. Moreover, the amino acids in vegetable proteins complement the amino acids absorbed from carbohydrates, so boosting their assimilation by the body (for example pasta and beans, rice and peas, cereals and lentils). In addition, vegetable proteins do not produce large amounts of metabolic waste and so place less strain on organs like the liver and kidneys. If you wish to reduce the intake of carbohydrates, you can eat proteins of animal or vegetable origin at both lunch and dinner. It is advisable, however, to do this at most 2-4 times a week and never for too long a period.
Carbohydrates are an essential food group for our organism. It should be remembered, however, that to keep your ideal weight and avoid altering the glucid metabolism, you should first of all choose complete carbohydrates from organic foods. It is also important to moderate the quantity eaten at a time, so as to allow your body to burn and use up the calories ingested without having to store them in the form of fat.
The ideal way to restrict or reduce glycemia is to always combine vegetables with carbohydrates, so the fibers interact with the sugar molecules and reduce the amount absorbed by the intestine. This means lunch will consist of:
• crudités/vegetables either raw or cooked;
• carbohydrates combined with vegetable proteins (legumes, soybean and derivates);
• or vegetable proteins alone;
• or animal proteins alone.

Dinner: a delicate meal

By now you will have realized that those who want to lose weight will have to change some of their eating habits: first of all what time they have dinner and what they eat.
At night we burn far fewer calories than during the day: we only need calories to keep the heart beating, the lungs working, the body temperature constant, etc....
If dinner is too rich in calories or eaten too close to bedtime, the surplus calories will be stored directly in the form of energy during the night. But if we have a light dinner, during the night we will draw on our reserves and so lose weight. For this reason it is important to have a light, healthy dinner, eating food that our bodies are unable to store. The ideal is to eat lean proteins, whether animal or vegetable, and calorie-free fibers, which have a

filling effect. This enables the body tissues to repair and regenerate themselves. So dinner should consist of:

- vegetables, steamed or grilled; minestrone or a soup of strained vegetables;
- animal or vegetable proteins.

Fish is preferable (at least 2 or 3 times a week), and the group of white meats.

Dominique Chenot's hints

Making amends after a lapse

- If you went off track ... you can always make amends! This book does not try to lay down a diet, so the rules it suggests are not rigid guidelines which demand sacrifices and cause frustration. A little indulgence is all to the good. Let yourself go as long as you know how to get your body back on target.
- The principal rule is a quick response. After enjoying a hearty dinner or plenty of wine, you have to give your body a break with a day of detox based on vegetable soups.
- In the case of real excesses, it will take three days to fix the problem. The body itself has various recovery systems. Just give it time and the elements it needs to trigger a response. Just three days of fruit and vegetables, water and a little brown rice will purify the system.
- Respecting the three-day interval each month for short detox cycles means doing a 36-day diet in the arc of the year: a really good result.

phytotherapy in the kitchen

Research in the service of wellness

Quick, simple, effective. If you're short of time, away from home or you simply don't feel like cooking, the dietary products of Chenot's food line will help you get your daily intake of high quality freeze-dried protein in the form of yogurts and beverages. A healthy meal in a single shot. Simply complete it with the addition of vegetables and fresh fruit. The extraordinary qualities of efficiently absorbed HP protein, discovered by the Biontology Laboratory, is the basis of the Chenot food line. It ensures perfect assimilation by the body, promoting a feeling of satiety. In addition, a 200 ml portion of creamy lyophilized soup contains the equivalent of 120 grams of vegetables cooked with the traditional method. And remember that freeze-drying is a technology that preserves the organoleptic properties of the vegetables and fruit used in a product without preservatives, added flavors or dyes. These soups do you a world of good. They enable you to maintain your muscle mass (even better when combined with regular exercise), fight osteoporosis and help you lose any extra weight by homing in on fats, not muscle mass or bone density.

Ingredients for culinary phytotherapy

Apple Intestinal regulator. Antiseptic and purifying. Contains copper, arsenic and bromine.
Artichoke Cleanser and diuretic. Helps prevent disorders of the liver, kidney and circulation.
Asparagus Diuretic Contains bromine.
Carrot Recommended for eyesight and the complexion. Strengthens the bladder. Acts on the endocrine glands. Contain calcium.
Celery Useful against mineral deficiency. Contains bromine. Recommended in slimming diets.
Dandelion Useful in combating high cholesterol levels, obesity and cellulite.
Dried beans Rich in protein. Strengthen the nervous system. Contains iron.
Garlic Cardiac stimulator (activates the circulation). Contains sulfur, arsenic and bromine. Assists digestion. Prevents microbial proliferation. Recommended against intestinal parasites.
Grapes Contain sugars not harmful to diabetics. Beneficial in cases of heart disease, hypertension and rheumatism. A source of copper and bromine.
Leek Reinforces the vocal cords. Effective against rheumatism. Combats atherosclerosis and obesity. Diuretic. Contains copper and bromine.
Nuts Contain magnesium (beneficial to the nervous system and the calcium balance) plus calcium, phosphorus and copper.
Onion Eaten raw it stimulates diuresis. Rich in vitamins A, B, C, iron, calcium, phosphorus, potassium, sodium, sulfur, iodine, silicon and sugars, all assimilated easily by the body.
Soy A complete food. Rich in proteins.
Spinach Rich in minerals. Its iron and magnesium have tonic and restorative effects, acting on the central nervous and sympathetic system as well as the muscular apparatus. Also contains calcium, copper and arsenic.
Turnip Strengthens the organism, contains copper, arsenic, calcium.
Watercress Rich in iron. Contains carotene, vitamins A, B1, B2, C, E, PP, and sulfur. An antidote to nicotine for smokers. Important in reintegrating minerals.

Chinese medicine

Chinese medicine, at the center of the program of treatment developed at the Espace Henri Chenot, is based on a division into 5 elements, each associated with a color, a natural element, a season, two organs or functions, an emotion and a taste. These elements interact continually in a cycle of destruction and another cycle of construction, with effects on the corresponding organs. Here are the colors and their correspondences:

- Green element, wood, spring, liver and gall bladder, anger = sour taste
- Red element, fire, summer, heart and small intestine, pleasure = bitter taste
- Yellow element, earth, late summer, stomach and spleen, reflection = sweet taste
- White element, metal, autumn, lungs and large intestine, sad = pungent taste
- Gray element, water, winter, kidneys and bladder, fear = salty taste.

Clearly all tastes are allowed or even required, while avoiding excesses. For example: a little pungent food stimulates the lungs and intestines, but an excess causes liver stress. A little sugar (preferably the kind that is absorbed slowly, such as the sugar in fruit, vegetables, legumes and whole grains) stimulates the pancreas, but too much harms the kidneys causing water retention and cellulite.

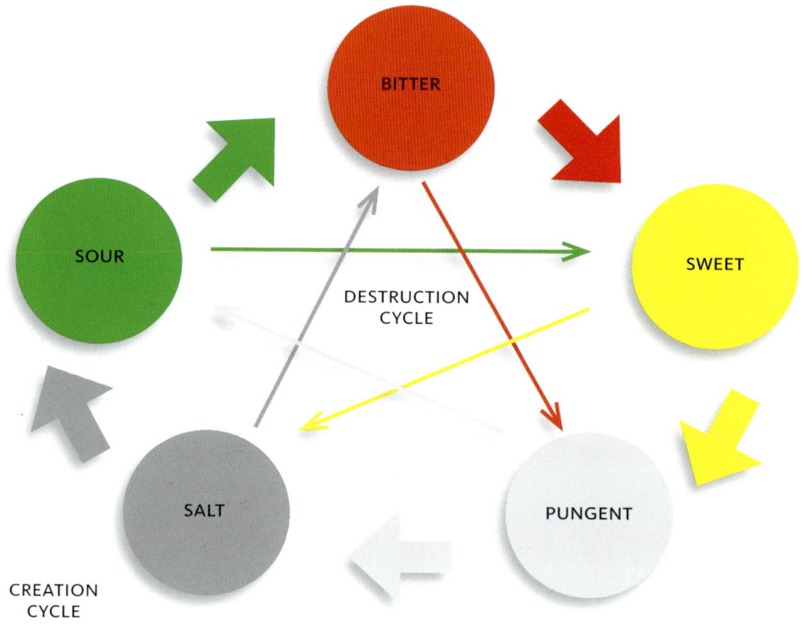

The five elements

Green Element

Organ	Disorder	Fruit and vegetables
Liver	Swelling	Asparagus, carrots, chicory, dandelion, olive oil, grapefruit, radishes, blackcurrants
	Congestion	Watercress (drainage), turnip (drainage) celery, gooseberries
	Hepatic impairment	Asparagus, artichokes, carrots, ribs of celery, lemons, rhubarb, radishes, soya
Gallbladder	Dysfunction	Carrots, olive oil
	Infection	Watercress
	Gallstones	Dandelion, tomatoes, grapes

Red Element

Organ	Disorder	Fruit and vegetables
Heart	Disorders of circulation of the blood	Chestnuts, garlic, lemon, parsley, rye
	Heart fatigue	Onions, pomegranates, turnips, celery, grapes
	Acidic blood and humors	Onions, strawberries, peaches, tomato (juice), grapes
	Purification of the blood	Asparagus, sorrel, artichokes, cucumbers, lemons, radishes, turnips, celery
	Hypertension	Garlic, lemons, pears, parsley, currants, rice, rye
	Hemolysis	Garlic, cabbage, lemons, tomatoes
Small Intestine	Inflammation	Seaweed, loquats
	Infections of the intestine	Apples, blueberries, tomatoes, pumpkin
	Intake of minerals	Carrots, cabbage, chestnuts, dates, cherries, strawberries, nuts, wheat germ, lettuce, lentils, almonds, apples, leeks, turnips, celery, soy, spinach, grapes, all cereals

Yellow Element

Organ	Disorder	Fruit and vegetables
Stomach	Inflammation, irritation	Apples, tomatoes, currants, grapes
	Atony	Garlic, pineapple, chicory, ribs of celery, apples, grapefruit, rhubarb
	Digestive spasms	Lettuce
	Lymphatic drainage	Watercress
Spleen	Inflammation	Asparagus, beetroot, chicory, blackcurrant
Pancreas	Atony	Eggplant

White Element

Organ	Disorder	Fruit and vegetables
Lungs	Disorders	Cabbage, watercress, quince, strawberries, apples, melons, turnips, radishes, celery
Bronchial tubes	Disorders	Garlic, seaweeds, horseradish, radishes, turnips
	Drainage of the respiratory tract	Figs, turnips
Large intestine	Constipation	Seaweed, sorrel, cherries, melons, blackberries, olive oil, pears, prunes, currants, pumpkin, grapes
	Drainage of the intestinal tract	Figs
	Regulator of intestinal functions	Loquats

Classification of foods according to the five flavors

	Pungent	Sour
Organs	Lungs Large intestine	Liver Gall bladder
Cereals	Fresh Oats	Wheat
Legumes	Whole wheat bread	Green beans
Vegetables	Garlic, raw onions, pickled gherkins watercress, parsley, horseradish, raw turnip, radishes	Sauerkraut, tomatoes, spinach
Fruit	Walnut, ginger	Apricots, ginger, sour cherries raspberries, sour apples, blackberries, blueberries, plums, currants, grapes
Various		

Gray Element

Organ	Disorder	Fruit and vegetables
Kidney	Weakness	Oats, chicory, dandelion, ribs of celery, apples, muskmelon, turnips, salsify, celery, grapes
	Drainage	Radishes, pumpkin
	Urea	Oats, artichokes, cranberries, tomatoes, grapes
	Uric acid	Cucumbers, onions, green beans, strawberries, raw beetroot juice, grapes
	Kidney stones	Chickpeas, dandelion, lemons, apples, pears, tomatoes, leeks, grapes
	Increase in urine acidity	Avocado
	Stimulant	Cauliflower
	Urinary retention	Raw bean juice: ½ a cup a day in severe cases

Sweet	Salty	Bitter
Stomach, spleen, pancreas	Kidneys, bladder	Heart Large intestine
Corn, barley, rice		Buckwheat, millet
Lentils, peas, soy	Borlotti beans	
Carrots, cooked onions, seaweed, cooked kale, cooked turnips, pumpkin	Seaweed, sauerkraut vegetables pickled in brine	Dandelion, endive, nettle, leek
Dried fruits (except apricots), dessert apples, pears, peaches, plums		Bitter orange
Vinegar, lemon, yogurt		Fish, sea salt

ingredients and cooking methods

Ingredients

The recipes in this book include some ingredients that may not be known to everyone. They are used in a dietetic cuisine to enhance the flavor or texture of foods and sauces, without doing the least harm to health, and often adding positive benefits to already healthy dishes. Other ingredients are quite common and in everyday use. Taken together, they are extremely useful to create a balanced and varied diet.

Apple cider vinegar

Description Made by fermenting apple cider. Air comes into contact with the yeast, turning the cider into vinegar.
Properties Rich in potassium, facilitates the elimination of liquids and therefore has a diuretic and detoxifying effect. Stimulates digestion and relieves pain in the joints and arthritic problems.
Recommended dose 2 to 3 spoonfuls per liter of water.
Use Dissolved in 1 liter of water it makes a good drink throughout the day.

Agar-agar

Description Powdered extract from certain kinds of red seaweed used as a thickening agent in foodstuffs. Consists of 80% fiber.
Properties Its texture helps give consistency to food ingested in the stomach, imprisoning some of the sugars and fats, so preventing them being absorbed by the body. Also very rich in iron.
Recommended dose Up to 3 grams per person per day.
Use Must be diluted in water before being added to a dish.
Special features A basic ingredient of various traditional dishes in Japan. Every spring, in particular, it returns to center stage when it comes to weight loss.
Dissolved in soup or a hot drink taken before a meal agar-agar will help you lose weight even if your eating habits are unchanged.

Seaweeds

Hijiki Often sold ready to use, otherwise it should be washed in sea water and then cooked in water for at least 3 hours until it all the liquid is absorbed.
Kombu Widely used in cooking. Use it as a side dish with vegetables, or add it to soups, broths or with rice. Must be left to soak until it becomes soft, then cooked.
Nori Mainly used in sushi.
Wakame Also very common. Must be soaked for 5-10 minutes and then cooked briefly.

Amaranth

Description Not a cereal in the strict sense, but used as such. It is a member of the Chenopodiaceae (goosefoot family) and is gluten-free.
Properties Contains valuable proteins that complement those contained in cereals, legumes, nuts and seeds. Has twice as much iron as wheat and four times as much calcium.

Oat bran

Description Oat bran is the outer layer that protects the oat seed. It consists of fibers that can absorb 25 times their weight in water, creating a unique hunger breaker. It cannot be digested because the body does not have the enzymes needed to use it.
Properties Thanks to these powerful features, oat bran:
• captures part of the calories absorbed, substances which are then evacuated in the stool without being digested
• carries away the toxic waste that in the long term would harm the body
• lowers blood sugar, because it does not pass through the blood, so preventing a sense of hunger, drowsiness and weight gain
• cuts cholesterol levels
• it is considered an anti-cancer food because it protects the walls of the colon from contact with the products of synthesis.
Recommended dose Not more than 4 spoonfuls per day per person.
Use Bran is used in making pastry bases for tarts which are crisp but free from fats. It can also be used in making dough for pies, clafoutis gratin, crumble, blinis, crepes, focaccia, muffins, cookies.

Glucomannan

Description A gelling fiber with a high hydration rate. Extracted from the tuber of Amorphophallus konjac, a plant of the widespread Araceae family. Indigenous to Vietnam, it is now cultivated from Indonesia to Japan and China. The tuber is cooked, then chopped, dried and ground to a fine white powder.
Properties Glucomannan is a soluble fiber that resembles psyllium, but with greater absorbent and soothing properties. Contact with water increases its volume 17 times, so a small quantity suffices to obtain the benefits normally attributed to these fibers: regulation of intestinal transit times, lowering of fat levels in the blood and better glucose control. Glucomannan has very low caloric and glycemic indices. In addition, because it swells up in water, in the intestine it forms a viscous mass of gel that hinders the absorption of nutrients. This makes it particularly suitable for low-calorie diets.
Recommended dose Varies with the preparation and consistency of the product.
Special features This flour is a basic ingredient in Asian cuisine, used to make various kinds of noodles, including shirataki in Japan. (There the flour is used to make a kind of gelatin called konnyaku, firmer than tofu but presented in the same way and with similar kitchen uses.)

Kamut

Description Kamut is an ancient variety of wheat, of great nutritional value, cultivated 5000 years ago in the Fertile Crescent from ancient Egypt to Mesopotamia.
Properties A source of micronutrients (potassium, phosphorus, calcium, etc.), the kamut kernel is two to three times the size of the wheat kernel and contains from 20% to 40% more protein. It is also richer in amino acids and essential fatty acids. Its magnesium and zinc content makes it an excellent anti-fatigue food. Like spelt and rye, cereals with an equally ancient tradition, kamut is a good alternative to wheat for people with intolerance to gluten.

Recommended dose Quantities are the same as for wheat.
Use Kamut is available in grains, like bulgur, in semolina, in flakes, as puffed grains, in some types of muesli or in the form of pasta. It is also used to make various types of confectionery or pastries.
Special features Suitable for eliminating toxins and purifying the blood; recommended in case of arthritis, anemia, skin diseases and stomach disorders.

Kuzu and arrowroot

Description These are foods with healing properties and very similar to each other, being used as thickeners for hot or cold preparations. Kuzu is a thickening agent extracted from the root of a Japanese plant. Arrowroot is a starch, also extracted from the root of a plant (Maranta arundinacea), which is reduced to a fine white powder and similarly used for thickening soups, sauces, etc.
Properties Excellent digestives which alleviate minor inflammations. Also known for their qualities as muscle relaxants
Recommended dose Varies according to the method and consistency of the preparation.
Use Available in powder or crystal form and should always be diluted in a little water before use as an ingredient.
Special features Can be used to thicken a vegetable soup or prepare desserts made from fruit or vegetable milk (for example in a flan), to bind a sauce, in breading, etc.

Oil

Description Most vegetable oils have about the same energy value: 30 ml of oil contain 28 grams of lipids.
Properties Their characteristics vary as a function of their composition. Though oils have the same energy value, they do not contain the same types of fatty acids:
• palm oil and coconut oil should be avoided as far as possible. They are rich in harmful saturated fatty acids that directly increase cholesterol levels
• olive, canola, peanut, avocado, hazelnut and almond oil are all rich in Omega 9 monounsaturated fatty acids
• canola and peanut oil, like safflower, corn, linseed, walnut, sesame, soybean and sunflower oil, are rich in polyunsaturated fatty acids sourced exclusively from our diet because the body is unable to produce them itself (Omega 3 and Omega 6). The oil with the highest concentration of Omega 3 is linseed oil.
Recommended dose The ideal would be to combine two types of oil in the same dressing, so as to benefit by the fatty acids they contain. Variation is therefore essential with a basic dietary ingredient such as oil. An oil spray is a practical and economical way of using oil sparingly. Another key parameter in the use of oils is their temperature (see below).
Use Each oil has a critical temperature (or smoke point) which should not be exceeded, because its components them become degraded and toxic. Some oils, such as walnut, which has a low critical temperature, should not be used in cooking. Discard any oil that has reached its smoke point.
Peanut and olive oil are best for cooking and can be used interchangeably because they lose their flavor.

Special features
Critical temperature or smoke point of:

- peanut oil 232°C (refined), 160°C (unrefined)
- canola oil 204°C (refined), 107°C (virgin)
- olive oil 242°C (refined), 216°C (virgin), 191°C (virgin)
- sunflower oil 232°C (refined), 107°C (unrefined).

As a term of comparison, butter has a smoke point of 150°C.

Quinoa

Description A sacred plant of the Incas. Unlike rice and wheat, not a grass but a "pseudo-cereal." It belongs to the chenopods, a plant family which includes spinach and chard.
Properties Quinoa is becoming better known because it contains large amounts of high quality protein, polyunsaturated fatty acids and many micronutrients, in particular magnesium, iron and potassium. Due to its nutritional composition, which is rather different from other cereals, and its flavor, its inclusion in the diet makes it possible to vary the menu. Gluten-free, it is much appreciated by those allergic to this substance.
Recommended dose From 20 to 30 grams of raw quinoa correspond to about half a cup of quinoa when cooked (125 ml).
Use Quinoa can be used in many ways: it can be sprinkled on a gratin or used to stuff vegetables. It can be consumed on its own or with a dish of vegetables, it can be eaten as a hot dish or a salad. Finally, it can be the basis for desserts.

Red Rice

Description Derived from a fungus that grows on rice. This fungus ferments and produces a red pigment called red yeast rice. Hence it is not the rice that is red but the pigment, which gives the rice its distinctive color.
Properties Red yeast rice, available as a food supplement or consumed together with the rice, is well known for lowering cholesterol, preventing heart disease and stimulating circulation of the blood.
Dose The rice is used in the usual amounts; the red rice beads as desired, since they are food supplements.
In the Far East red yeast rice has been used for centuries. It is beneficial consumed regularly or taken as beads or in other forms as a food supplement in cases of hypercholesterolemia.

Agave syrup

Description A natural sweetener, honey-colored, derived from the sap of a Mexican plant.
Properties It is a high-intensity sweetener with a low glycemic index (GI) and neutral flavor which facilitates its use. It contains large amounts of fructose, which yields a higher sweetening power than, for example, honey but with GI 4 or 5 times lower.
Recommended dose 150 grams of agave syrup replace 200 grams of sugar.
Use It is used in many preparations, hot or cold. It can also be used in cooking lacquered or sweet-and-sour meat or shrimps.

Stevia

Description A plant native to Paraguay which has long been used by the Guarani people.
It has been studied for over a century because of an exceptional property: it has the extraordinary sweetening power of sugar without its drawbacks.
Properties Low in calories, it has a sweetening power 300 times greater than industrial sugar. Tiny quantities are therefore sufficient to sweeten coffee or yogurt.
Recommended dose Divide the quantity of sugar by 300 to get the dose of stevia that suffices to replace it.
Use Stevia can be cooked and added to hot dishes (clafoutis, tarts, etc.) instead of sugar, unlike aspartame, for example.

Ginger

Description This fragrant root can be used fresh or dried. Ginger is rich in minerals but poor in sodium, hence particularly suitable in a salt-free diet.
Properties Ginger is credited with many medicinal qualities:
- aids digestion
- reduces nausea
- its antioxidants help prevent heart disease and some forms of cancer
- valued as an aphrodisiac.

Recommended dose Everything depends on the strength of the flavor desired in a dish. As with all spices, doses are very subjective.
Use The ginger rhizome should be firm, compact, not dry, light brown in color with a pale yellow pith, juicy and fragrant. It should not be wilted, faded or mildewed. It can be used fresh (diced or grated), dry (powdered), candied, as a spice, seasoning or dessert.

Other ingredients

Vegetable stock cubes are better than stock cubes of animal origin because they contain no waste products such as animal fats and purines, but vegetable fats, spices and flavorings. Prefer monopodial vegetable stock cubes free from glutamate, or those with sea salt.
Miso A vegetable sauce widely used in China and Japan. It consists of a fermented mixture of soy, rice or wheat, salt, water and vegetable aromas (nuts and vegetables). The fermentation is due to Aspergillus oryzae, which breaks up the complex protein, lipid and glucid molecules into easily digestible products. Miso is used to make broths and soups.
Tamari A very tasty sauce of oriental origin. It is a savory product used to flavor vegetables, fish, meats and soups. To be added after cooking.

Cooking methods

Here is a list of cooking methods which brings out their good and bad points. A very important note about meat: the longer it cooks, the more difficult it is to digest and the more it tends to cause putrefaction in the intestine which is toxic to the organism.

Oils and fats should also be cooked as little as possible, otherwise they become toxic. For vegetables and fish, the same principle applies: cook them lightly so as not to lose their nutrients.

Boiling or steaming

The longer the cooking time the greater the nutrient loss. We recommend using as little water was possible and waiting till it boils before adding vegetables or seaweed. Cooking with a pressure cooker, being more rapid, is useful to preserve vitamins. The water used to soak or cook vegetables and seaweed can be used for soups or broths, or to cook cereals and legumes, so recovering the lost minerals. In the case of steaming the food is not brought into contact with the water so losses are reduced.

Baking and roasting

These cooking methods does not require large amounts of fat because the heat quickly creates a protective crust which keeps all the nutrients in the food. Cooking in the oven frees the fats which drain into the pan in the form of gravy (to be eliminated). Baking foods by wrapping them in aluminum foil is the supreme method of cooking. The aluminum forms a protective barrier that prevents the loss of nutritional elements like vitamins and minerals while retaining heat and the flavors of foods.

Microwave cooking

With this method, the heat spreads quickly into the food, the degradation of vitamins is limited and the food does not become dehydrated. The latest generation of microwave ovens pose no great problems, although they should be used only occasionally for defrosting or heating food. In fact it is not a true method of cooking: certain cultures of bacteria survive and may be dangerous, especially in the case of milk or products for babies.

Cooking in foil

An excellent method. The vitamins and minerals are not dispersed but remain in the food, whose nutritional value is fully preserved. Some examples are fish baked in foil with vegetables or fillets of lean meat with vegetables. The cooking is quite rapid and does not require the addition of fat.

Sous-vide

This is low temperature cooking in a vacuum, which fully preserves the qualities of foodstuffs. It can be used to cook any type of food: fruit, vegetables, fish and meat. The procedure is simplicity itself. First carefully place the food in the bag. This is then placed in the device which creates a vacuum and the open end of the bag is sealed. The bags containing the food in a vacuum are then placed in a steam oven or a pan containing water at a temperature between 65 and 98°C, depending on the type of food to be cooked. When cooking is complete, the bag is opened with a pair of scissors and the dish prepared.

Barbecuing

Beware of burning wood and coal, which can lead to the formation of toxic compounds. If meat fats or other foodstuffs turn black it indicates hyper-oxidation of the fats and the presence of harmful saturated fats.

Frying

To be used rarely or never, if possible. In any case take care to use oils resistant to heat and with a high smoke point, such as peanut oil. Never use the same oil twice. Plain olive oil is not recommended; only extra virgin olive oil has a smoke point of 230°C and is therefore advisable for frying. Never exceed 180°C: above this temperature the alteration of fats is toxic.

Wok

This is a sort of deep pan, hemispherical and made of carbon steel or cast iron. It has the advantage of keeping the heat even and spreading it over the whole surface. It is important for the flame it is heated on to be as large as the diameter of the bottom of the wok, so as to form a very hot zone from which the heat spreads all over the rest of the wok. It can be used for steaming or sautéing ingredients. For steaming there are baskets In which to rest the food and cook it in a natural way.

Recipes

salads and starters

Bavaroise of artichokes

4 SERVINGS

8 artichokes
20 g scallions
1 garlic clove
2 spoonfuls extra virgin olive oil
juice of one lemon
1 glass white wine
500 ml vegetable stock
1 spoonful fresh thyme chopped
1 spoonful parsley chopped
4 leaves Swiss chard
8 leaves white celery
lemon zest
flakes of parmesan cheese
unrefined sea salt
milled black pepper

Remove the outer leaves of the artichokes, cut off the tips with a knife and scrape the hard part of the stem. Cut the artichokes into quarters and leave them to soak in water acidulated with the juice of half a lemon. Lightly brown the chopped scallion and garlic in the extra virgin olive oil, add the artichokes but keep 4 of the quarters for a garnish. Add the white wine and let it evaporate over a high flame, then add the stock and let it evaporate over lower heat.
Cook for 20 minutes. Remove from the hob and blend coarsely, flavor with the unrefined sea salt, pepper, thyme, parsley and the rest of the lemon juice.
Blanch the 4 Swiss chard leaves, lay them on a work surface and cut out some circles with a diameter of about 10 cm. Fill a mold with a diameter of 8 cm with the artichoke and turn out onto the leaf of Swiss chard.
Garnish with the white celery leaves, a quarter of artichoke, lemon zest, and some flakes of parmesan cheese.

Thai salad

4 SERVINGS

1 Iceberg lettuce
100 g soybean sprouts
1 cucumber
1 carrot
1 bunch fresh coriander
10 mint leaves
2 sprigs lemon grass
50 g mixed cress
For Oriental sauce see recipe on p. 129

Use the 4 outer leaves of the lettuce as 4 baskets. Julienne the rest of the lettuce. Add the soybean sprouts. Finely julienne the cucumber and carrot and mix them with the cut salad, then add all the other herbs. Dress the salad at the last moment and serve in the lettuce baskets. Garnish with the cress.

Mixed salad vegetables and diced tofu grilled with lime vinaigrette

4 SERVINGS

400 g of mixed salad vegetables
200 g of tofu with beet greens
50 g walnuts, broken
chives
For lime vinaigrette
see recipe on p. 134

Prepare the vinaigrette. Trim the salad vegetables and arrange them on a dish. Add the diced and lightly grilled tofu, the walnuts and the chives. Pour over the vinaigrette.

Red and white cabbage with arugula and apples

4 SERVINGS

1 head medium-sized white cabbage
1 head medium-sized red cabbage
20 red cherry tomatoes
2 small bunches of arugula (rucola)
1 red apple
50 g pumpkin seeds

For the dressing
500 ml vegetable stock
2 bay leaves
1 spoonful cumin
1 onion
1 garlic clove
200 ml apple vinegar
100 ml extra virgin olive oil
unrefined sea salt

Cut the cabbages into thin strips using a sharp knife. At the same time bring the vegetable stock to a boil with the bay leaves, cumin, onion and garlic, salt and simmer gently for about 15 minutes. Strain the liquid through a sieve and use it, still warm, to dress the cabbage, also adding the vinegar and extra virgin olive oil. Leave for at least 10 minutes. Garnish the salad with the tomatoes cut in halves, the arugula and the red apple sliced finely and the pumpkin seeds.

Our pinzimonio in an eastern version

4 SERVINGS

4 rice sheets (available in Oriental specialty shops)

12 tender new carrots

8 leaves radicchio

4 leaves Belgian salad

4 scallions, cut

lengthwise

8 young wild asparagus

4 fennel hearts

2 stalks white celery

Chinese Enoki mushrooms

fresh pea sprouts

For the green sauce see recipe on p. 131

Soak the rice sheets for 10 minutes in cold water. Meanwhile peel and slice the vegetables. Divide them into four portions and arrange in the rice sheets shaped into cones. Serve, if desired, with green sauce.

Agar-agar of tomatoes and artichokes

4 SERVINGS

400 g tomato puree
1 vegetable stock cube
2 spoonfuls agave syrup
3 g agar-agar powder
300 g cleaned artichokes
½ lemon
1 spoonful gomasio
1 spoonful chopped tarragon
1 spoonful sea salt
2 spoonfuls spelt bread crumbs
4 spoonfuls black olive paste or green sauce
10 snow peas or green beans, boiled
4 sprigs tarragon

Simmer the tomato purée with the vegetable stock cube and agave syrup for 10 minutes.
Add the agar-agar and continue cooking a few minutes longer. Combine for a few seconds in the mixer. Pour the sauce into a pan and cover it with plastic film. Leave it in the fridge for a few hours.
Clean, wash and halve the artichokes, simmer them in salted water in which you have placed half a lemon. Cool and pass through a vegetable mill (medium disk).
Season the artichoke puree with the gomasio and chopped tarragon, add the sea salt and spelt bread crumbs.
Cut the agar-agar into equal-sized rectangles, sprinkle them with the artichoke puree and roll up each rectangle.
Serve the rolls of agar garnished as desired with the olive paste, the cooked snow peas or green beans and the sprigs of tarragon.

Sicilian-style eggplant au gratin with tofu

4 SERVINGS

2 long eggplants
1 bunch fresh thyme
2 cloves garlic
1 spoonful extra virgin olive oil
fresh herbs to taste
20 pumpkin seeds
For light pesto see the recipe on p. 129

For the filling
2 tomatoes, peeled and diced
1 small red bell pepper
10 taggiasco olives
10 green olives
10 capers
100 g smoked tofu
10 leaves fresh oregano
1 spoonful sambal oelek
sea salt
2 spoonfuls extra virgin olive oil

Wash and cut the eggplants in half lengthwise. Place them in an oven dish so they rest on the peel and score the pulp in a crisscross pattern about 1 cm deep. Sprinkle with fresh thyme, garlic cooked in oil and parsley, a spoonful of extra virgin olive oil, and then bake at 180°C for 20 minutes.
Peel the tomatoes, remove the seeds and dice. Dice the bell pepper. Add the olives, capers and tofu.
Mix all the ingredients, then season with oregano, sambal oelek, sea salt and two spoonfuls of extra virgin olive oil.
Gratinate in the oven at 200°C for about 5 minutes. Garnish with the light pesto sauce and pumpkin seeds.

Cooked vegetables with tofu and tomato sauce

4 SERVINGS

100 g carrots

100 g green and yellow zucchini

100 g Romanesco broccoli

100 g cauliflower

100 g cleaned and trimmed artichokes

100 g shiitake mushrooms

100 g green beans

100 g asparagus

100 g broccoli

sea salt

20 leaves of coriander and tarragon

2 spoonfuls extra virgin olive oil flavored with basil (or sesame oil or walnut oil)

4 banana leaf baskets (available from Oriental specialty stores)

whole chive stems

For the tofu sauce

2 ripe tomatoes

100 g tofu

100 g tofu velouté

1 vegetable stock cube

½ spoonful mustard

1 spoonful white miso

Simmer the vegetables separately in salted water or steam them. Each vegetable has its own cooking time. Chop the coriander and tarragon roughly. For the tofu sauce: blanch and peel the tomatoes, cut them into quarters and remove the seeds. Then combine all the ingredients in the blender. For the presentation of the dish, use 4 banana leaf baskets, fill them with tofu sauce, not too cold. Serve the cooked vegetables piping hot with the banana leaf basket containing the tofu sauce beside them. Add the chives and season with basil oil, sesame oil, or walnut oil as desired.

Beetroot ravioli

4 SERVINGS

2 large red beetroots

200 ml water

3 spoonfuls balsamic vinegar

1 celeriac

3 spoonfuls apple cider vinegar

20 pea shoots

1 small head of curly lettuce

4 spoonfuls cream of balsamic vinegar, white or black

1 spoonful black sesame

For the filling

100 grams cashew nuts

20 g white miso

100 ml millet milk or rice milk

2 spoonfuls chopped fresh herbs (thyme, coriander, parsley)

Soak overnight the cashews with the miso and millet milk (or rice milk). Then mix them together to make a thick cream and add the chopped herbs.
Peel the beetroot and cut into 20 thin slices, then marinate them in a little water with balsamic vinegar for a few hours. Peel the celeriac and julienne into narrow strips, then marinate it with the apple cider vinegar.
Fill the beetroot with the cream of cashew nuts and close each slice to form the ravioli.
Arrange the ravioli on the plates and garnish with the julienned celery root, cream of balsamic vinegar, pea sprouts, curly lettuce leaves and black sesame.

Tabbouleh

4 SERVINGS

150 ml vegetable stock
100 g bulgar of barley or of buckwheat
2 tomatoes
1 small cucumber
3 spring onions
2 small bunches parsley
2 small bunches mint
20 g toasted pine nuts
1 red onion
5 spoonfuls lemon juice
4 spoonfuls extra virgin olive oil
sea salt
freshly ground pepper
1 small head of green lettuce

Pour the piping hot stock over the bulgur, cover the pan and wait until the broth is completely absorbed by the bulgur.
Meanwhile wash, peel and roughly chop the vegetables and herbs, add the toasted pine nuts and season the whole with lemon juice, oil, salt and pepper. Let it rest for about 15 minutes.
Serve the tabbouleh in a single dish with the bulgur or separately. Garnish as desired with the lettuce leaves.

soups

Detox Soup

4 SERVINGS

150 g leeks
1 onion
2 red peppers
1 head of green cabbage
1 spoonful corn germ oil
1 ½ liters water
2 vegetable stock cubes
1 spoonful kuzu
1 lemon
chives

Clean and pare the vegetables, cut into chunks and fry in a spoonful of corn germ oil for 1 minute. Add the water and vegetable stock cubes and cook for at least 30 minutes.
Blend the soup and pass it through a sieve.
If the soup is too liquid thicken it with a teaspoon of kuzu dissolved in a little water.
Add the lemon juice and garnish with the chives.

Vegetable stock

4 SERVINGS

1 onion
1 carrot
1 leek
1 turnip
1 heart of green celery
1 fennel bulb
1 clove garlic
4 shiitake mushrooms
1 vegetable stock cube
(or some sea salt)
1 spoonful chopped parsley
1 stalk lemongrass
50 g of kombu
bay leaf

Grill the unpeeled onion on a wire rack till it turns a fine golden color and then tip it into a pot of simmering water.
Add all the vegetables pared and washed, the vegetable stock cube (or sea salt) and simmer over medium heat for about 1 hour.
Turn off the heat and add the parsley, lemon grass, seaweed and bay leaf to obtain an infusion.
When the stock has cooled filter it and discard the vegetables. The liquid thus obtained can be stored in ice cube trays in the freezer for use in sauces, risottos and much else.
To use it as vegetable stock you can add the juice of a fresh lemon or fresh ginger juice or a pinch of pepper, according to taste.

Cream of broccoli soup

4 SERVINGS

500 g green broccoli, chopped
1 onion
1 garlic clove, crushed
1 bay leaf
1 l vegetable stock
1/2 glass white wine
1 spoonful extra virgin olive oil
1 spoonful kuzu (or arrowroot)
4 spoonfuls natural yogurt

In a saucepan with a thick base brown the onion and garlic in the oil together with the bay leaf for about 3-4 minutes. Add the broccoli, setting aside some tips for a garnish, the stock, and the white wine. Bring to the boil and simmer gently for 10 minutes. Remove the bay leaf and allow to cool. Purée in a blender and adjust for salt.
Warm the mixture, again over a low heat, thickening if necessary with the kuzu or arrowroot. Meanwhile simmer the broccoli tips till they are tender (8-10 minutes). Cool them in running water. Sprinkle them over the soup and make a pattern with the whisked yogurt just before serving.

Cream of chestnuts with oil of truffles

4 SERVINGS

400 g chestnuts precooked
1 onion
1 potato (or 1 teaspoon kuzu)
1 spoonful of extra virgin olive oil
1 l vegetable stock
1 spoonful truffle oil
1 or 2 Brussel sprouts
sea salt (or vegetable bouillon cube)

Lightly brown the onion in the oil, add the potato peeled and diced, the chestnuts, vegetable stock, sea salt or vegetable bouillon cube. Gently simmer for about 30 minutes, then purée in the blender and keep warm. Meanwhile, remove the leaves from the Brussel sprouts and sauté them in a non-stick pan. Pour the cream of chestnuts into a bowl and garnish, as desired, with the leaves of the sprouts and truffle oil.

Cream of artichoke soup

4 SERVINGS

6 large artichokes
(if necessary, use 600 g
of frozen artichokes)

100 g onions

1 garlic clove

1 dl white wine

1 l vegetable stock

1 sprig thyme

1 spoonful kuzu

chives

Simmer the chopped onion and garlic in the white wine till soft. Add the artichokes, peeled and cut into pieces, and the thyme and vegetable stock. Cover and simmer gently for about 20 minutes. Remove the thyme, purée the whole in a blender to obtain a smooth cream and sieve the mixture. If the cream is too thin, thicken it with the kuzu. Decorate, if desired, with the chives.

Jerusalem artichoke soup

4 SERVINGS

200 g Jerusalem artichoke

2 medium-sized potatoes

1 garlic clove

1 onion

1 teaspoon extra virgin olive oil

1/2 glass white wine

1 l vegetable stock

50 g adzuki beans
(soaked for at least 6 hours)

1 spoonful walnut oil

chervil

sea salt (or vegetable bouillon cube)

Simmer the adzuki beans in the water they have soaked in for at least 30-40 minutes.
Peel and cut up the Jerusalem artichokes—keeping a little for the garnish—and the potatoes. Chop the garlic and onion and brown them lightly in the oil, then add the white wine, Jerusalem artichokes, potatoes, and the vegetable stock. Flavor with the salt or vegetable bouillon cube and simmer gently for about 20 minutes. Purée in a blender.
Finely slice the Jerusalem artichoke set aside before and grill the slices in a non-stick pan until they are lightly colored.
Pour the soup into bowls and garnish with a spoonful of adzuki beans, some slices of Jerusalem artichoke, a few drops of walnut oil and the chervil.

Cream of pumpkin scented with vanilla

4 SERVINGS

700 g pumpkin
2 small onions
2 vanilla pods
300 ml soybean milk
700 ml vegetable stock
1 spoonful corn germ oil
1 pinch of powdered chili
kuzu (or arrowroot)

Cut the onion into large slices. Peel and dice the pumpkin. Cut the sticks of vanilla in two lengthwise. Brown the onions in a spoonful of oil, add the diced pumpkin and brown for 5 minutes more. Pour in the soybean milk and vegetable stock and add the vanilla.
Cover and simmer gently for about 30 minutes. Remove the vanilla and purée in the blender. Add the chili. If the cream is too thin, thicken it with kuzu or arrowroot dissolved in water.

Cold melon soup with ginger

4 SERVINGS

2 melons
1 spoonful extra virgin olive oil
1 teaspoon grated ginger
fresh ginger, cut in strips
fleur de sel

Peel the melons and blend them with the oil, grated ginger and a pinch of salt.
Pour the soup into bowls and garnish with the fresh ginger strips.

Summer minestrone of tomatoes and fruit

4 SERVINGS

4 ripe San Marzano tomatoes
1/4 of a ripe pineapple
12 strawberries
2 spoonfuls balsamic vinegar
extra virgin olive oil
a pinch of fleur de sel
green of fennel
2 strawberries for the garnish

Peel and seed the tomatoes, purée them in the blender with the balsamic vinegar and the fleur de sel and put the mixture in the refrigerator. Cut the pineapple into cubes of about 1 cm per side and prepare the strawberries by cutting them to the same size as the pineapple. Pour the tomato soup into bowls and arrange the fruit on it. Decorate with the strawberries and green of fennel and add a few drops of extra virgin olive oil.

first courses and vegetable protein dishes

Polenta gnocchi with tomato and pesto concassé

4 SERVINGS

500 ml soy milk or oat milk
500 ml water
1 vegetable stock cube
250 g cornmeal
2 spoonfuls extra virgin olive oil
2 spoonfuls sesame oil
4 spoonfuls light pesto
(for the recipe see p. 129)
4 spoonfuls tomato concassé
(for the recipe see p. 127)
100 g cooked adzuki beans
4 basil leaves

In a saucepan simmer the soy milk (or oat milk) with the water and vegetable stock cube, then slowly pour in the polenta, stirring steadily with a whisk. If it is too thick add more water. Cook the polenta over low heat, stirring with a wooden spoon for about 30 minutes.
When cooked, add the olive oil and sesame oil. Allow to cool for about 20 minutes and then use the pastry bag to form strips of about 20 cm in length. Allow to cool for a further 20 minutes, then cut the strips to a width of 3 cm to make the gnocchi.
Sauté the polenta gnocchi in a nonstick pan with the pesto, tomato concassé and azuki beans. Garnish with the basil leaves.

Whole wheat lasagnette with broccoli and cauliflower

4 SERVINGS

For the pastry

100 g Whole wheat flour

100 g plain flour

100 g semolina of durum wheat

2 eggs

2 spoonfuls of extra virgin olive oil

100 ml warm water

1 coffeespoon tamari

salt

For the vegetables

1 medium-sized broccoli

1 cauliflower

For vegetable béchamel sauce see recipe on p. 127

Mix the different kinds of flour. Add the eggs, oil, water, tamari, and salt. Knead into a smooth dough. Stand in the refrigerator for about 30 minutes. Roll the dough out thin and cut out rectangular pieces (ca. 15 x 7 cm). Simmer in salted water for a few minutes and cool them in iced water.
Cut the vegetables into small pieces. Steam cook for a few minutes.
Prepare the béchamel; when it is ready, grease a pan with extra virgin olive oil, pour in a layer of béchamel, then add a layer of the lasagna and then one of vegetables, repeating the sequence till all the ingredients have been used.
Bake the lasagna for 25 minutes at 175°C.

Brown rice spaghetti

4 SERVINGS

1 carrot

1 green or yellow zucchini

250 g of brown rice spaghetti
whole sea salt

5 Brussels sprouts

4 spoonfuls tomato purée

4 spoonfuls light pesto
(for the recipe see p. 129)

2 spoonfuls basil flavored olive oil

4 red basil leaves

Julienne a carrot and a zucchini and cook the rice spaghetti for 7-8 minutes in lightly salted water.
In the last 3 minutes add the carrots first and then the zucchini, julienned into strips.
Drain the spaghetti when still slightly al dente.
Meanwhile warm the purée with the tomato and pesto and spread it on the plates, then add to the spaghetti. Season with basil-flavored olive oil and garnish with the red basil leaves.

Semi-whole grain risotto with saffron and confit of cherry tomatoes

4 SERVINGS

300 g semi-whole grain rice
1 onion
1 spoonful peanut oil
1 dl white wine
1 liter vegetable stock
1 sachet saffron
2 spoonfuls extra virgin olive oil
saffron pistils
fresh herbs

For the cherry tomato confit
20 cherry tomatoes
20 g chopped shallots
2 teaspoonfuls peanut oil
40 g spelt bread crumbs
30 g dried tomatoes
1 spoonful gomasio
thyme, rosemary, tarragon, chopped
1 spoonful agave syrup
1 teaspoonful garlic powder

Wash the tomatoes and cut in half. Place them with the cut side up on the bottom of a pan lined with baking paper. Sauté the chopped shallot in the peanut oil, remove from the heat still warm, add the bread crumbs, the dried tomatoes chopped, the gomasio, toasted sesame seeds and chopped thyme, rosemary and tarragon, agave syrup and garlic powder.
Mix everything together and pour the mixture over the cherry tomatoes.
Cook in the oven for 2 hours at 85°C.
For the risotto, sauté the onion in the peanut oil for a few minutes, pour in the white wine and let it evaporate. Add two ladles of hot vegetable stock and stir well with a wooden spoon. When it is nearly evaporated, add more stock little by little; when half cooked pour in a sachet of saffron and add more stock as needed until cooked.
Remove the pan from the heat and make the risotto creamy by adding two spoonfuls of extra virgin olive oil.
Serve the risotto with the accompanying cherry tomato confit and garnish it with the saffron pistils and fresh herbs.

Oriental Rice

4 SERVINGS

200 g brown basmati rice
20 g fresh or frozen peas
20 g carrots
20 g snow peas
20 g shiitake mushrooms (or field mushrooms)
20 g zucchini
20 g pumpkin
20 g pak-choi (Chinese cabbage)
20 g broccoli
1 teaspoonful coriander
1 small bunch parsley
1 small bunch green mint
2 spoonfuls yellow curry paste
2 spoonfuls sesame oil
4 spoonfuls tomato purée
fresh herbs
black garlic in flakes

For the turmeric sauce
150 ml coconut milk
150 ml rice milk
1 stalk lemongrass
1 spoonful fish sauce (available from Oriental food stores)
1 spoonful white miso
1 spoonful turmeric
1 spoonful kuzu

Simmer the basmati rice for 30-40 minutes. Wash and chop all the vegetables to the same size and simmer them in lightly salted water.
Chop the coriander and mint leaves, reserving a few for garnish. Then mix the rice with the vegetables, parsley and mint. In a saucepan, or better still a wok, brown the yellow curry paste in sesame oil, add the rice with the vegetables and sauté them together for a few minutes.
Meanwhile prepare the turmeric sauce by simmering the coconut milk and rice with the chopped lemongrass, fish sauce, miso, white miso and turmeric for about 15 minutes over low heat. Then bind with the kuzu dissolved in water. Pass through a sieve.
Fill some molds with the mixture and serve with the turmeric sauce and tomato purée. Garnish with a few leaves of fresh herbs and black garlic flakes.

Basket of basmati rice and wild rice with carrot sauce

4 SERVINGSS

120 g whole basmati rice

40 g wild rice

4 rice sheets
(available in Oriental specialty shops)

vegetable stock

160 g of mixed vegetables cut in lozenge shapes (Savoy cabbage, carrots, zucchini)

4 teaspoons of extra virgin olive oilvegetable stock

chopped parsley (or chives)

For carrot sauce see recipe on p. 132

To make baskets from the rice sheets: soak them in cold water for 5 minutes, drain and put on the outside of 4 crème caramel molds, so that they take their shape. Bake them in the oven at 170°C for about 10 minutes and leave to cool.
Boil the basmati rice for 25 minutes and the wild rice 40 minutes in the vegetable stock: drain and set aside.
Boil the vegetables in vegetable stock for the cooking time of each: the vegetables should be cooked but not soft.
Warm the rice, mix with the vegetables and dress with the extra virgin olive oil.
Fill the rice baskets with the rice and vegetables, put one on each plate, pour over the carrot sauce, sprinkle, if desired, with chopped parsley or chives, and serve.

Quinoa cooked in the wok with vegetables and ginger

4 SERVINGS

4 rice sheets (available from Oriental specialty shops)
250 ml vegetable stock
200 g quinoa
30 g peas
1 bunch of chervil
1 sprig of tarragon
30 g chopped shallots
1 spoonful peanut oil
30 g carrots, diced
30 g celery, diced
30 g zucchini, diced
30 g red bell pepper, diced
2 spoonfuls fresh ginger juice
1 spoonful sesame oil

For the artichoke sauce
4 artichokes, cleaned
500 ml vegetable stock
1 teaspoonful fresh ginger juice
juice of ½ lemon
1 spoonful ginger juice
1 spoonful extra virgin olive oil

Prepare the baskets by immersing the rice sheets in cold water for about 5 minutes. Drain them and wrap them around the outer walls of 4 pudding molds to take the shape. Bake them in the oven at 180°C for about 10 minutes and allow to cool.
Meanwhile, cook the chopped artichokes in vegetable stock with the juice of ½ lemon for about 15 minutes. Combine all the ingredients in a blender and add the ginger juice and olive oil. Pass through a sieve.
Bring the broth to a simmer, add the quinoa and cook over low heat for about 15 minutes with the lid on. Drain the quinoa and set aside.
Simmer the peas, chop the chervil and tarragon and set aside. Sauté the shallots and diced vegetables for a few minutes in peanut oil in the wok over a low heat, then add the quinoa, peas, ginger juice, sesame oil, chopped herbs and continue until everything is well browned.

Risotto of emmer wheat and barley with herbs and black olive sauce

4 SERVINGS

100 g emmer wheat

250 g barley

1 medium-sized onion

2 l concentrated vegetable stock

sweet herbs
(chives, mint, basil, parsley, coriander)

1 spoonful tamari

1 teaspoon white miso

2 spoonfuls extra virgin olive oil

For black olive sauce see recipe on p. 133

Soak the emmer wheat and barley for 2-3 hours, then wash them carefully. Stew the onion in a little of the vegetable stock then add the two cereals and the rest of the stock. Simmer gently until the liquid is absorbed. Then add the herbs chopped fine, the olive oil, tamari and miso.
Serve the risotto with the black olive sauce.

Millet cracker with baked vegetables and tamari sauce

4 SERVINGS

150 g millet
(soaked for 5 hours)

1/2 l soybean milk

1 vegetable bouillon cube

1/2 sachet saffron

nutmeg

thyme, marjoram, basil, coriander

1 spoonful white miso

4 slices of fresh pineapple

For the tamari sauce see recipe on p. 130

Baked vegetables

1 carrot

1 zucchini

1 white turnip

3 roots Hamburg parsley
(or 1 purple potato)

1/2 celeriac

1/2 red bell pepper

1 fennel

1-2 spoonfuls walnut oil

Simmer the milk together with the drained millet and the vegetable bouillon cube. Add the saffron and nutmeg and simmer over gentle heat for about 20 minutes, stirring all the time. When cooked, add the chopped herbs and the miso.
Leave to cool in a baking dish and then shape as desired. Grill in a non-stick pan at moderate heat.
Peel and cut the vegetables into small lozenges and bake them in the oven at 200°C for about 20 minutes, turning them every so often. When done dress with the walnut oil and serve with the millet cracker.
Grill the slices of pineapple to taste and accompany the dish with the tamari sauce.

Vegetable strudel

4 SERVINGS

For the pastry
150 g plain flour
150 g Whole wheat flour
3 teaspoons extra virgin olive oil
1 egg
100 ml lukewarm water
unrefined sea salt

For the filling
2 carrots
2 fennel
1 celeriac
3 artichokes
1 eggplant
2 zucchini
2 spoonfuls oil scented with basil
1 spoonful sesame oil
10 leaves basil
3 spoonfuls amaranth
unrefined sea salt or white miso (or gomasio)

For the garnish
100 g black olives, pitted
1 garlic clove
2 spoonfuls of tomato sauce

Mix all the ingredients together to obtain a dough that is supple but not soft. Cover it and let it stand for about 20 minutes. Peel the vegetables, julienne them or cut them into small pieces and bake them in an oven at 180 C° for about 15 minutes. Allow them to cool and dress them with the oil scented with basil or sesame oil, the basil leaves cut into strips and the salt (or miso or gomasio).
Roll out the dough as thin as possible, flouring if

necessary. Arrange the vegetables on the sheet of dough and roll them up together. Put the strudel on an oven tray using the oven paper and brushing it with the sesame oil. Pop the amaranth in a warm non-stick pan with the lid on for about 30 seconds and then cover the strudel again. Bake in an oven preheated to 175°C for about 25 minutes.
Slice the strudel while hot and serve, if desired, with a tapenade of black olives made by puréeing the olives and the clove of garlic in a blender into a soft cream. Accompany with the tomato sauce.

Light leek pies with green olives and tomato concassé

4 SERVINGS

For the pastry
100 g plain flour
100 g emmer wheat flour
50 ml lukewarm water
2 spoonfuls extra virgin olive oil
unrefined sea salt

For the filling
1 leek cut into lozenges and blanched in boiling water or steam
250 ml soybean milk
2 eggs
1 spoonful of gomasio
10 leaves fresh coriander, chopped
1 spoonful miso
100 g green olives, pitted
For tomato concassé see recipe on p. 127

In a bowl, mix the sifted flower, water, oil and sea salt. Knead them until you have a smooth, stiff dough. Stand in the refrigerator for at least 30 minutes. Roll out the dough into a thin sheet and cut out 4 disks. Brush oil on 4 pie molds and line them with the pastry.
Mix all the ingredients with the soybean milk. Add the filling until it is half a centimeter from the edge and bake at 170°C for about 20 minutes. Remove from molds, decorate as desired and serve with a spoonful of tomato concassé and the sauce of olives, made by puréeing them in a blender for a few seconds. If desired, a little vegetable stock can be added to make it creamier.

Whole grain crêpes with spinach

4 SERVINGS

For the crêpes

50 g spelt flour type 0

50 g whole grain spelt flour

250 ml soy milk

2 eggs

½ a vegetable stock cube

a few spoonfuls of milk

nutmeg

1 teaspoonful extra virgin olive oil

For the filling

250 g of fresh spinach

50 g of tofu

½ a vegetable stock cube

1 spoonful gomasio

1 spoonful tamari

1 spoonful miso

2 spoonfuls spelt bread crumbs

200 ml tomato purée

200 ml béchamel sauce
(for the recipe see p. 127)

Mix all the ingredients for the crêpes to make a rather liquid paste. Cook the crêpes in a non-stick skillet and lay them flat on the work surface.
Cut out some discs with a diameter of about 12 cm. Wash and trim the spinach, blanch it in lightly salted water, pass it through the vegetable mill with the chopped tofu, then dress it with the stock cube mixed with a little water and the gomasio, tamari, miso and bread crumbs. Spread the spinach purée on the crêpes, roll them up and cut into strips at least 4 cm wide. Place them in a terra cotta dish lined with tomato purée and cover with the hot béchamel sauce. Bake for 10 minutes at 180°C.

Spicy bulgur with bell pepper sauce

4 SERVINGS

200g bulgur of barley or spelt
250 ml vegetable stock
10 g pine nuts
10 g pumpkin seeds
10 g pistachios
10 g cashew nuts
10 g raisins
1 small bunch dill
1 small bunch coriander
10 g mixed spices
(cardamom, turmeric, cumin, curry)
2 spoonfuls walnut oil
juice of 1 lime
4 baby peppers
fresh herbs

For the bell pepper sauce
400 g yellow peppers
1 shallot, finely chopped
1 spoonful corn oil
500 ml rice milk or millet milk
1 vegetable stock cube
1 teaspoonful turmeric
1 spoonful kuzu

Bring the broth to a simmer, add the bulgar of barley (or spelt) and cook over a low heat for about 15 minutes with the lid on. Remove from heat and cool the bulgur, stirring occasionally with a wooden spoon.
Meanwhile, in a non-stick pan toast the pine nuts, pumpkin seeds, pistachios, cashews and raisins till golden.
Chop the dill and coriander roughly and add the herbs and spices to the bulgur, mixing everything well.
Sauté the shallot cut into julienne strips in the corn oil, add the yellow bell peppers, trimmed and cut into small pieces, and continue cooking for a few minutes, then pour the milk (or millet) rice, a spoonful of miso, the vegetable stock cube and turmeric. Bake for 20 minutes.
Combine all the ingredients with an immersion blender. Dissolve the kuzu in a little water and whip in with the sauce to bind the ingredients.
Sauté the bulgur in a skillet or wok with the walnut oil and add the lime juice.
Serve the bulgur in a soup dish with baby bell peppers filled with the yellow pepper sauce and leaves of fresh herbs.

Vegetable couscous

4 SERVINGS

40 g whole couscous
350 g ripe tomatoes
200 g pumpkin
200 g zucchini
1 small bell pepper
1 carrot
1 turnip
3 artichokes
2 cardoons (in season)
2 onions
4 garlic cloves
extra virgin olive oil
3 vegetable bouillon cubes dissolved in 1.5 l water
200 g of tomato paste
3 teaspoons powdered spices (ginger, saffron, turmeric)
1 packet tofu
fresh coriander, chopped
30 g pine nuts, roasted
30 g raisins
1 spoonful tamari
a handful of cooked chickpeas
juice of 1 lemon

Prepare the couscous according to the instructions on the packet.
Peel the vegetables. Cut into matchsticks the pumpkin, the zucchinis with their skin, the bell pepper and the carrot. Prepare the artichokes by removing the tough outer leaves and dipping the hearts of the artichokes in water acidulated with lemon juice. Prepare the cardoons in the same way. Chop the onions and 3 small garlic cloves and brown them in a little extra virgin olive oil, add the vegetable stock, tomato paste and 1 teaspoon of powdered spices. Simmer over a low heat and add all the vegetables, beginning with the toughest

(turnip, bell pepper, carrot) and continuing to simmer for about 1 hour. Add the chickpeas. Meanwhile prepare the balls of soybean with the tofu puréed in the blender. Add one chopped clove of garlic, the 2 teaspoonfuls of powdered spices, the chopped fresh coriander and roasted pine nuts and the raisins. Mix the ingredients and shape the mixture into small meatballs. Grill them till they are a golden color.
This couscous is served in three dishes or individual bowls: one containing the stock, one the vegetables and the balls of soybean, and one the couscous.

Bulgur burger

4 SERVINGS

250 of buckwheat bulgur

1 vegetable stock cube

100 g natural tofu

100 g smoked tofu

20 g diced celery

20 g diced carrots

mixed herbs
(coriander, dill, oregano, chervil)

1 spoonful sesame oil

For the sweet and sour sauce, see recipe on p. 129

Pour the bulgur into at least 300 ml of water. Add the vegetable stock cube and simmer gently in a covered pan for about 15 minutes, until water is fully absorbed. Remove from the heat and allow to cool. Add the two types of tofu sliced and the diced celery and carrots with the mixture of chopped herbs and sesame oil. Mix well and form into burgers. Cook on the grill or in a skillet for a couple of minutes. Serve with caponata or the sweet and sour sauce.

Tofu and seitan patties

4 SERVINGS

150 g tofu

100 g seitan

1 vegetable stock cube

10 g pumpkin seeds

10 g sunflower seeds

10 g pine nuts

30 g carrots

2 spoonfuls mixed herbs

1 spoonful gomasio

spelt bread crumbs or oat bran (optional)

1 spoonful sesame oil

For the red sweet and sour sauce see recipe on p. 130

Pass the tofu, seitan and vegetable stock cube dissolved in water through the vegetable mill to produce a purée. Toast the pumpkin seeds, sunflower seeds and pine nuts in a skillet.
Blanch the julienned carrots. Chop the mixed herbs, add the gomasio and add the whole mixture to the purée of tofu and seitan. Knead the mixture, adding breadcrumbs or oat bran if necessary, until you can form it into patties.
Fry in a pan with a spoonful of sesame oil for a couple of minutes. Serve with the mushroom sauce or vegetables sautéed in the wok and garnish with sweet and sour red sauce.

Black soybean patties with celery sauce

4 SERVINGS

200 g black soybean (soaked for 5-6 hours)

5 leaves of Savoy cabbage

10 field mushrooms

10 chanterelles or other mushrooms

1 vegetable bouillon cube

1 onion

1 garlic clove

30 g breadcrumbs

1 spoonful whole wheat flour

2 spoonfuls extra virgin olive oil

unrefined sea salt

For celery sauce and red turnip sauce see recipes on p. 133

Prepare the red turnip sauce. Cook the beans for 30 minutes in the same water in which they were soaked. Roughly chop the Savoy cabbage and mushrooms. Chop the onion and garlic and brown them in 2 spoonfuls of extra virgin olive oil, add the Savoy cabbage and the mushrooms. Continue to simmer for some minutes, then leave to cool. Purée in a blender half the quantity of the beans together with a few spoonfuls of their cooking water in which a bouillon cube has been dissolved. Then knead them together with all the other ingredients: the onions and garlic with the cabbage and mushrooms, breadcrumbs, whole wheat flour, and unrefined sea salt. Allow to stand for about 1 hour, then shape the mixture into patties. Roast the patties delicately on the grill or in a non-stick pan. Purée the celery sauce in the blender and spread it on the plates, arrange the patties on it and garnish, as desired, with the red turnip sauce.

Patty of grilled scented tofu

4 SERVINGS

300 g tofu

1 l vegetable stock

2 spoonfuls pumpkin seeds
and pine nuts, roasted

2 spoonfuls gomasio

2 spoonfuls whole wheat breadcrumbs

1 spoonful herbs
(thyme, marjoram, tarragon)

1 spoonful miso

powdered garlic or ginger

tomato sauce (optional)

Simmer the tofu in the vegetable stock for 10 minutes, then allow to cool. Put the cooked tofu in the cutter and add all the other ingredients. Purée all the ingredients in the blender for 15 seconds, adding 2 spoonfuls of vegetable stock, till they form a smooth mixture. Shape it into patties and cook them on the grill or non-stick pan.
If desired, they can be served with a tomato concassé or vegetable ragout.

Roulades of eggplant stuffed with soybean noodles

4 SERVINGS

200 g fine (or medium-sized) soybean noodles

2 green zucchini

2 yellow zucchini

2 eggplants

1 spoonful miso

chervil

coriander

200 ml tomato sauce

unrefined sea salt

For vegetable béchamel see recipe on p. 127

Simmer the soybean noodles 4-5 minutes in abundant salted water, drain and allow them to cool. Meanwhile, julienne the green and yellow parts of the zucchini and sauté them in a non-stick pan. Cut the eggplants lengthwise into slices about half a centimeter thick and grill them without oil. Chop the vegetables, chervil, and coriander and use them together with the miso to dress the noodles. Spread the filling over the slices of eggplant and roll them into roulades.
Pour some tomato sauce into a cocotte and arrange the roulades on it. You can also pour some vegetable béchamel over the roulades.
Bake them at 170 °C for about 10 minutes.
Serve in the cocotte.

animal protein dishes

Rack of lamb with pistachio crust

4 SERVINGS

800 g rack of lamb
2 spoonfuls peanut oil
2 cloves of garlic
fresh herbs
(rosemary, thyme, sage)
freshly ground pepper
1 spoonful mustard
120 g of chopped pistachios
30 g of spelt bread crumbs
salt
300 g fresh peas
1 dl vegetable stock
2 spoonfuls of soy cream
2 red onions, already steamed

Marinate the lamb for a day in the oil, garlic, herbs and pepper. Cool it in the refrigerator.
Remove the lamb from the refrigerator, drain the meat and cook it lightly on the grill or skillet.
Over the still hot meat pour the mustard, chopped pistachios, spelt bread crumbs and salt. Bake at 185°C for 15 minutes. Allow it to rest for 5 minutes, then slice the rack. Meanwhile, cook the peas in salted water, blend with the vegetable stock and soy cream and season with salt. Serve the meat with the peas puréed and pieces of steamed red onions.

Veal in mustard crust

4 SERVINGS

700 g fillet of veal
1 sprig of thyme
1 sprig of rosemary
1 bay leaf
1 sage leaf
garlic powder
peel of ¼ of an untreated lemon
150 g mustard
150 g bread crumbs
salt
1 spoonful balsamic vinegar
1 spoonful extra virgin olive oil
freshly ground pepper

For the side dish
4 boiled artichokes
400 g mashed carrots
vegetable stock
2 spoonfuls olive oil
4 sprigs of tarragon

Put the meat sous-vide with all the herbs and keep it in the refrigerator for 24 hours. Then cook the meat sous-vide in its special bag for 5 hours at 54°C in a steam oven.
Cool in iced water. Remove meat from its bag and place on a baking tray. Cover the meat with the mustard and all the bread crumbs.
Bake at 180°C for 10 minutes.
Slice the meat and arrange the slices on a platter, accompanying it with the boiled artichokes, and purée of carrots previously made by steaming the carrots or simmering them in lightly salted water; then drain them and blend them together with the vegetable broth and 2 spoonfuls of olive oil. Drizzle with the balsamic vinegar, olive oil and pepper. Garnish with the sprigs of tarragon.

Turkey burgers

4 SERVINGS

500 g ground turkey breast

1 egg yolk

50 g of chopped eggplant pulp (cooked in the oven for 20 minutes at 190°C)

½ spoonful sambal oelek

4 g of black or white sesame toasted

1 spoonful chopped coriander

1 spoonful chopped chervil

2 spoonfuls spelt bread crumbs

1 spoonful gomasio

1 spoonful sesame oil

1 small onion, chopped and browned

1 eggplant

1 tomato

1 head of lettuce

In a bowl combine the ground turkey and mix all the ingredients until the mixture is smooth.
Form 4 burgers and cook over low heat in a nonstick skillet.
Meanwhile, cut the vegetables into slices and grill or cook in a nonstick pan for a few minutes until they are done.
Serve the burgers with the grilled vegetables and garnish with salad leaves.

Chicken with cloves of garlic and baked pumpkin

4 SERVINGS

1 chicken

2 onions

12-16 garlic cloves

1 spoonful ginger

2 sprigs of fresh thyme

3 spoonfuls fresh coriander

500 ml vegetable stock

2 spoonfuls extra virgin olive oil

a pinch of saffron

3 small cinnamon beans

1 spoonful lemon juice

100 g candied lemon

8 slices pumpkin baked in the oven at 180°C for about 10 minutes (or sautéd on the grill for some minutes)

8 steamed Brussels sprouts

unrefined sea salt

whole black pepper, milled

Wash the chicken, pat it dry with kitchen paper and singe it, then divide it in four. Peel and chop the onions, garlic, ginger, thyme and coriander. Put the ingredients in a saucepan together with the vegetable stock, extra virgin olive oil, saffron, cinnamon, and lemon juice. Add the pieces of chicken, adjust for salt and pepper and simmer over medium heat with the lid on for 45 minutes. Remove the pieces of chicken and reduce the cooking liquid. Remove the cinnamon beans, add the candied lemon and briefly sauté the chicken pieces, after removing the skin.
Serve hot with the slices of pumpkin.
In summer the pumpkin can be replaced by steamed zucchini or other vegetables grilled.

Turkey meatballs with turnip tops and bulgur wheat Oriental style

4 SERVINGS

400 g minced turkey
1 spoonful of powdered ginger
1 spoonful parsley, chopped
1 scallion, chopped coarsely
1 small carrot diced, sautéd in a non-stick pan
linseed oil
1 spoonful tamari
unrefined sea salt
red pepper, milled

Bulgur wheat Oriental style
400 g bulgur wheat
400 ml vegetable stock
1 red bell pepper

For the Meatballs
Mix all the ingredients with the minced turkey and knead together. Shape into meatballs and brown them in a non-stick pan with a little linseed oil.
If desired, add a spoonful of tamari during the cooking to make the meatballs darker.

1 onion

1 dried fig

3 dried apricots

1 spoonful of raisins
(previously soaked in warm water)

saffron

curry powder

paprika

powdered cumin

cinnamon

3 pieces of dried tomatoes (or in oil), chopped coarsely

1 lemon pickled in salt and chopped coarsely

2 spoonfuls pine nuts, roasted whole

5 black olives, chopped coarsely

3 spoonfuls fresh parsley, chopped

1 leek, chopped then steamed for 2-3 minutes

1 spoonful extra virgin olive oil

For the Bulgur wheat Oriental style
Brown the bell pepper and the chopped onion in the oil over medium heat and add the chopped dried fig, the chopped dried apricots, and raisins. Also add a knife-tipful each of saffron, curry, paprika, powdered cumin, and cinnamon.
Simmer the bulgur wheat about 20 minutes in the vegetable stock over a low heat. When cooked, add all the other ingredients, and lastly the seasoning. Serve the turkey meatballs with the bulgur wheat and garnish as desired.

Steamed pollock flavored with vanilla

4 SERVINGS

600 g of pollock cleaned and cut into 4 slices

1 bourbon vanilla bean divided into 4 pieces

4 teaspoonfuls extra virgin olive oil

4 teaspoonfuls fish stock (see recipe on p. 128)

For the fish sauce with cuttlefish ink

150 ml of fish stock

1 sachet cuttlefish ink

1 spoonful kuzu

For the side dish

400 g of green beans

100 g of dried tomatoes

2 spoonfuls extra virgin olive oil

1 spoonful roasted black sesame seeds

1 bunch coriander

sea salt

freshly ground pepper

Put the slices of pollock in a steam oven for a minute. Remove from the oven and allow to cool, then place them in four sous-vide bags with a piece of vanilla bean, olive oil (half a spoonful in each bag) and the fish stock.
Close the bags with the sous-vide machine and cook at 48°C in the steam oven for an hour.
Meanwhile, simmer the fish stock in the squid ink for a quarter of an hour, until it is reduced slightly. Bind with the kuzu dissolved in water.
Cook the green beans cut into equal lengths in salted water. When they are done cool them immediately under cold running water. Slice the dried tomatoes into julienne strips and mix with the beans. Then sauté the vegetables in a skillet of olive oil. Present the pollock on a bed of green beans with strips of tomatoes at the sides.
Garnish with the roasted sesame seeds and the coriander chopped roughly.

Stingray wings marinated with capers and herbs

4 SERVINGS

2 stingray wings weighing about 500 g each

1 onion

1 carrot

1 small bunch of parsley

1 rib of celery

2 bay leaves

1 dl of white wine

1 clove garlic

1 small bunch chervil

1 sprig tarragon

1 spoonful olive oil

For the black olive tapenade

100 g of taggiasco olives

20 g of capers

1 small bunch of parsley

1 spoonful mustard

1 clove garlic

1 spoonful extra virgin olive oil

2 spoonfuls of spelt bread crumbs

For the garlic cream

150 g silken tofu

1 spoonful garlic powder

1 spoonful of spelt bread crumbs

Cook the stingray wings by scalding them for about 15 minutes (more or less, depending on the size) together with all the spices.
Meanwhile, prepare the tapenade by finely chopping the olives, capers, garlic and parsley and then mix together the mustard, olive oil and spelt bread crumbs.
Remove the fish from the pan, trim it and serve warm with a tapenade of black olives and the garlic cream made by blending tofu, garlic and bread crumbs for a few minutes in the blender.

Squid noodles with sweet and sour sauce

4 SERVINGS

4 squid about 15 cm long, cleaned
1 carrot
1 zucchini
1 leek
1 clove garlic
2 spoonfuls extra virgin olive oil
100 g samphire
1 small bunch of coriander
1 small bunch of parsley
freshly ground pepper
sweet and sour sauce
(for recipe see p. 129)
squid ink sauce (for recipe see p. 108)

For the sweet and sour sauce
1 red pepper chopped
1 spoonful tomato paste
20 cl of rice vinegar
80 g of agave syrup
a pinch of sambal oelek
1 spoonful soy sauce
1 spoonful kuzu

To make the sweet and sour sauce: put the peppers together with all the ingredients and cook till done. Blend well, and if the mixture is too liquid, bind with kuzu dissolved in a little cold water.
Open the squid flat and cut into thin strips. Likewise trim and wash the carrot, zucchini and leek and cut them into strips for the "vegetable spaghetti."
Begin cooking the squid by sautéing them in the wok with the clove of garlic and oil, cook over high heat. Add the vegetable spaghetti and samphire, continue cooking for a few minutes longer, leaving the ingredients crisp.
Season with the coriander, parsley, salt and pepper. Pour a ladleful of sweet and sour sauce into the dish, add the spaghetti with the squid, and decorate around the dish with the squid ink sauce and serve. For a perfect result cook one portion of squid at a time.

Turbot with clams and samphire

4 SERVINGS

300 g of clams
2 cloves garlic
1 small bunch parsley
1 spoonful of whole coriander
and 1 spoonful of coriander finely chopped
½ liter of water
half dl white wine
1 spoonful fish sauce
2 spoonfuls extra virgin olive oil
600 g fillet of turbot cleaned
1 tomato, diced
30 g of samphire
4 leaves of pak-choi (Chinese cabbage)
4 sprigs of dill
sea salt
freshly ground pepper

Put the clams washed and cleaned in a sous-vide bag, add the garlic cut in half, a few sprigs of parsley and coriander, the mixture of water and wine, the fish sauce and 1 spoonful of olive oil.
Close the bag with the vacuum machine and cook in a steam oven for about 25 minutes at 85°C.
Remove from the oven, set aside the mussels and sieve the clam stock.
In a non-stick pan fry the turbot fillets in the remaining oil for 2 minutes per side, adding the stock made of clams, tomatoes and samphire.
Continue cooking for a few minutes until the sauce thickens slightly.
In the end add the clams, parsley and chopped coriander. Add salt and pepper as desired.
Serve the turbot with the pak-choi boiled or steamed or other vegetables to taste.
Garnish with sprigs of dill.

fruits and desserts

Pineapple ravioli

4 SERVINGS

1 pineapple

100 ml of green apple juice

50 ml balsamic vinegar

3 g kuzu

4 banana leaves (available from Eastern specialty stores)

4 mint leaves

poppy seed

strawberries

For the filling

300 g mango coulis

200 ml rice milk

20 g agave syrup

4 g agar-agar powder

15 g kuzu

½ vanilla bean

To prepare the mango coulis simply blend a ripe fruit weighing about 600 g.
Warm the rice milk with the mango coulis, agave syrup, agar-agar powder and add the vanilla.
Simmer the whole slowly for a few minutes then add the kuzu dissolved in a little water. Continue to simmer a few minutes longer.
Cool and put the mixture, which will serve as the filling, in the refrigerator for several hours until it thickens. Heat the apple juice and add the dissolved kuzu in a little water. Cut the pineapple into 20 thin slices. Arrange a little of the filling on it, close it so as to form pouches of ravioli and put it on the plates. Add the apple juice and balsamic vinegar, which should already have a fairly thick consistency.
Garnish with banana leaves and mint, poppy seeds and strawberries.

Coulis of fruit mosaic

4 SERVINGS

3 apples
200 g blueberries
(or blackberries)
200 g raspberries
2 ripe mangoes
2 ripe papayas
3 spoonfuls honey
5 teaspoons kuzu
4 leaves lemon balm (optional)

Peel and cook the fruit separately for a couple of minutes with a spoonful of honey and half a glass of water. If necessary thicken with a teaspoon of kuzu, previously dissolved in little lukewarm water. Leave to cool and then purée in a blender.
Strain the raspberries and blackberries (or blueberries).
Serve the individual coulis in dessert bowls and use a toothpick to create different patterns or designs, decorating, as desired, with leaves of lemon balm.

Yellow pears on a bed of redcurrants

4 SERVINGS

4 ripe Williams (Bartlett) pears

2 spoonfuls honey

800 ml applejuice
or centrifuged apple pulp

juice of 1 lemon

2 sachets saffron

coulis of blueberries
(see recipe on p. 116)

For the coulis of redcurrants

200 g redcurrants

100 ml apple juice

2 spoonfuls honey

1 teaspoon kuzu

Set aside a handful of the redcurrants for a garnish. Cook the rest with the applejuice, a little water and 2 spoonfuls of honey for a few minutes, thicken with the kuzu previously dissolved in a little lukewarm water, mix and then pass through a sieve.
For the pears, bring to a boil the apple juice and add 2 spoonfuls of honey, lemon juice, and saffron.
Peel the pears and simmer for about 10 minutes.
Line the dessert bowls with the redcurrant coulis and arrange the pears on them sliced into "fans."
Garnish with the redcurrants, if you wish, with some mint leaves and a coulis of blueberries.

Fruit agar-agar

4 SERVINGS

1 kg mixed berries
100 ml water
2 spoonfuls honey
20 g agar-agar

Cook the berries with water and honey for about 10 minutes. Blend and sieve them.
Add them to the prepared agar-agar diluted in a little water and continue cooking for another 2-3 minutes.
Put the mixture in pudding molds lined with plastic wrap and allow to cool for 5-6 hours in the refrigerator. Remove from the molds and serve on a platter garnished as desired.
As alternatives to berries, use mangos, papaya, apricots, peaches.

Quinoa with cranberries and coconut sauce

4 SERVINGS

150 g of quinoa
230 ml vegetable stock
150 g cranberries
2 spoonfuls agave syrup
1 spoonful kuzu
spelt bread crumbs (optional)
10 g chopped pistachios
4 spoonfuls of cream of balsamic vinegar
4 black bilberries
4 raspberries

For the coconut sauce
150 ml coconut milk
2 spoonfuls agave syrup
1 stalk lemongrass
juice of ½ a lime
1 spoonful kuzu

Cook the quinoa in vegetable broth with as much water as serves to cover it. Simmer over a low heat in a covered pot for about 15 minutes. When it has all been absorbed, leave it to cool. In a saucepan cook the cranberries with the agave syrup for a few minutes. If they are too liquid, thicken them with kuzu dissolved in a little water and allowed to cool. Add the quinoa with cranberries and mix together. If the mixture becomes too soft, add the spelt bread crumbs.
For the coconut sauce, simmer the coconut milk with the agave syrup, the lemon grass cut into pieces and the juice of ½ a lime for 10 minutes. Blend them all with the kuzu and allow to cool. To serve, spread the cream of coconut on the plates and form small cylinders of quinoa to place on the coconut sauce. Garnish with the black bilberries, fresh raspberries, cream of balsamic vinegar and sprinkle with the chopped pistachios.

Almond milk pudding with a raspberry coulis

4 SERVINGS

600 ml rice milk
3 spoonfuls almond syrup
2 spoonfuls honey
2 vanilla pods
1 spoonful kuzu
1 spoonful agar-agar
100 ml raspberry coulis
(see recipe on p. 116)
2 passion fruits
mint leaves

Bring to a boil the rice milk, almond syrup, honey, and one of the vanilla pods cut lengthwise. Thicken with the kuzu previously dissolved in a little lukewarm water and the powdered agar-agar. Simmer for 2-3 minutes more until you have a smooth, creamy mixture. Form layers of the almond milk pudding and raspberry coulis in glasses or glass bowls. Stand for 2-3 hours in a refrigerator. Decorate with the passion fruit pulp and the mint leaves.

Tofu sorbet with strawberries

4 SERVINGS

250 g strawberries
100 g white tofu
100 g red currants
500 ml rice milk
1 vanilla pod
1 teaspoon powdered agar-agar
3 teaspoons malt

Simmer the rice milk with the vanilla pod slit in 2 lengthwise. Add the agar-agar and dissolve slowly for 5 minutes over low heat; add the malt and allow the mixture to cool. Purée in a blender the strawberries and tofu and blend with the rice milk. Transfer the mixture to a bowl then put it in the freezer to set for at least 3 hours.
Before serving, purée the sorbet again to make it creamier and serve with red currants.

Duo of yin-yang sorbets

4 SERVINGS

For the pineapple sorbet
1/2 pineapple
2 spoonfuls acacia honey
100 ml rice milk
juice of 3 passion fruit, seeded

For the raspberry sorbet
300 g raspberries
2 spoonfuls orange-blossom honey
100 ml apple juice

100 g mango coulis
(see recipe on p. 116)
100 g blackberry coulis
(see recipe on p. 116)
100 g pine nuts
100 ml water
mint leaves

Purée the pineapple in a blender with all the ingredients and then do the same with the raspberries. Again separately, strain the two mixtures and use a sorbet-maker to produce two creamy sorbets. Put half a portion of the mango coulis in 4 dessert bowls and then add half a portion of the blackberry coulis. Serve the two sorbets with the mint leaves. If desired, use a purée of pine nuts and water to form the Tao symbol as in the image.

Mandarin and mango sorbet

4 SERVINGS

pulp of 2 ripe mangos

3 dl mandarin juice

1 spoonful of agave syrup

4 banana leaves

For the fruit salad

100 g pineapple

1 kiwi

1 pear

4 strawberries

100 ml of apple juice

juice of ½ a lemon

1 spoonful of bilberry coulis
(for the recipe for coulis see p. 116)

20 raspberries

20 blueberries

fresh mint leaves

Blend the mango pulp with the mandarin juice and agave syrup and immediately put in the sorbet-maker to produce the sorbet.
Prepare the fruit salad with the sliced fruit, apple juice and lemon juice. Serve the sorbet with the fruit salad and sliced strawberries on the banana leaf. Garnish with blueberries, raspberries, mint and the bilberry coulis.

sauces and dressings

Béchamel

4 SERVINGS

35 g spelt flour

35 g sunflower oil or olive oil

½ vegetable stock cube

½ liter of soy milk or oat milk

Mix the flour with the oil to make a soft compound. Dissolve the vegetable stock cube in the soy milk and warm the mixture over a low heat. Very gradually add them to the mixture, stirring steadily with a wooden spoon until the desired consistency is reached.

Vegetable béchamel

4 SERVINGS

1 liter soy milk

3 eggplants cooked in the oven at 200°C for about 20 minutes, then peeled and reduced to purée

nutmeg

1 vegetable stock cube

Simmer the soy milk, add the mashed eggplant, nutmeg and vegetable stock cube.
Continue cooking for a few minutes and then pass the mixture through a vegetable mill.
If the sauce is too liquid, thicken with arrowroot or kuzu.

Tomato concassé

4 SERVINGS

1 onion

1 clove garlic

½ cup white wine

5 San Marzano tomatoes diced

½ vegetable stock cube

2 spoonfuls extra virgin olive oil

10 basil leaves

Chop the onion and garlic and braise them in the white wine. Peel, seed and dice the tomatoes and add them together with the stock cube.
Cook for 10 minutes and then add the olive oil and chopped basil leaves.

Fish stock

4 SERVINGS

1.5 kg of fish carcasses (sole, turbot, red mullet, monkfish)
1 spoonful corn oil
1 onion
1 leek
1 rib of celery
½ fennel bulb
1 clove garlic
2 bay leaves
2 sprigs thyme
2 sprigs parsley
10 grains pepper
2 liters of water
250 ml of white wine
juice of ½ a lemon

Brown the onion, leek, celery, garlic and fennel all cut into pieces for a few minutes in a saucepan with corn oil. Add the fish carcasses, bay leaf, thyme, parsley and peppercorns. Continue cooking for a few minutes stirring steadily with a wooden spoon, then add water, white wine and lemon.
Over low heat cook the stock for about 40 minutes, occasionally skimming off any foam that forms while cooking. Pass the mixture through a sieve.
Keep the fish stock (fumé) in the refrigerator or freeze it in small containers.

Yellow curry paste

4 SERVINGS

1 small onion
2 cloves garlic
1 spoonful curry powder
1 spoonful turmeric
1 teaspoonful cardamom
1 vegetable stock cube dissolved in water
1 teaspoonful fresh tarragon
10 g fresh ginger
1 teaspoonful coriander powder
1 teaspoonful cumin
3 spoonfuls sesame oil

Combine all ingredients in a blender for a few minutes.

Light pesto

4 SERVINGS

3 small bunches basil
1 small bunch parsley
3 spoonfuls extra virgin olive oil
2 cloves of garlic
100 ml vegetable stock
10 g pine nuts
1 spoonful of Parmesan cheese
sea salt
chili or ginger

Blend all ingredients in a blender for a few minutes.

Sweet and sour sauce

4 SERVINGS

2 spoonfuls honey
3 spoonfuls rice vinegar
2 spoonfuls tamari
1 teaspoonful white miso
1 pinch of powdered ginger
1 dl of water
kuzu (optional)

Simmer all the ingredients for about 20 minutes, whisk well and continue cooking for another 3 minutes. If necessary, thicken with kuzu.

Oriental sauce

4 SERVINGS

1 lime
1 clove garlic
1 fresh red chili
1 teaspoonful honey
2 spoonfuls fish sauce
2 spoonfuls rice vinegar
3 spoonfuls extra virgin olive oil

Combine all ingredients in the mixer and pass the sauce obtained through a strainer.

Oriental hummus sauce

4 SERVINGS

60 g boiled chickpeas

½ clove garlic or 1 teaspoonful garlic powder

20 g of tahina (sesame cream)

10 g lemon juice

10 g ginger juice

100 g vegetable broth

2 g vegetable stock cube

1 teaspoonful chopped chervil

1 spoonful sesame oil

Combine all the ingredients in a mixer for a few minutes and then add the chopped chervil and sesame oil.

Red sweet and sour sauce

4 SERVINGS

200 ml of water

3 spoonfuls rice vinegar

3 spoonfuls of honey

2 red bell peppers, peeled and chopped

1 stalk lemongrass, chopped roughly

50 g of grated ginger

1 spoonful tomato paste

1 spoonful arrowroot (optional)

Simmer all ingredients for about 20 minutes, mix well and continue cooking for another 3 minutes. If necessary, thicken with arrowroot.

Tamari sauce

4 SERVINGS

50 ml tamari

50 ml water

1 spoonful kuzu

1 pinch chili powder

Dissolve the kuzu in the water and thicken over the heat.
Add the tamari and chili.
Mix well and allow to cool.

Green sauce

4 SERVINGS

2 green bell peppers
1 onion, cooked in wine
1/2 cup white wine
300 ml vegetable stock
1 spoonful fresh ginger juice

Cut the bell peppers into small pieces and add to the onion previously braised in the white wine. Add the vegetable stock and simmer for about 15 minutes, whisk well and pass the sauce through a sieve. Add the ginger juice.

Wok sauce

4 SERVINGS

20 g oyster sauce
20 g strong soy sauce
2 g sesame oil
2 g agave syrup
25 g cold mushroom stock or vegetable stock
2 g sambal oelek
1 clove garlic
1 pinch powdered or fresh ginger

Combine all the ingredients in a mixer for a few minutes to make a fairly liquid sauce.

Avocado sauce

4 SERVINGS

1 ripe avocado
2 spoonfuls extra virgin olive oil
2 spoonfuls apple cider vinegar
1 spoonful tamari
1 teaspoonful strong mustard
mixed herbs
vegetable stock

Whisk all the ingredients for a few minutes, add the amount of vegetable stock required to make a rather liquid sauce.
Using the same procedure, instead of avocado, various kinds of cooked vegetables can be used (carrots, asparagus, artichokes, tomatoes).

Avocado and turmeric sauce

4 SERVINGS

1 clove garlic
1 fresh red chili
1 teaspoonful turmeric powder
juice of 2 Granny Smith apples
juice of 1 lemon
1 spoonful extra virgin olive oil
1 ripe avocado

Finely chop the garlic and chili and add the turmeric powder. Combine the the orange, apple and lemon juice, and reduce the amount to one third by simmering. Cool and mix with the extra virgin olive oil and pulp of the avocado.
Sieve and keep cold.

Carrot sauce

4 SERVINGS

1 glass carrot juice
1 teaspoonful miso
1 teaspoonful kuzu

Reduce the carrot juice to half over low heat, add the miso and bind with kuzù while simmering for 2 minutes.

Soy bean sauce

4 SERVINGS

1 onion
2 spoonfuls sesame oil
120 g of soy beans dried (soaked in water overnight)
800 g ripe tomatoes, peeled and seeded
700 ml vegetable stock
2 bay leaves
2 teaspoonfuls sambal oelek
kuzu or arrowroot

Brown the onion in the sesame oil, add the drained soybeans, tomatoes and vegetable stock.
Adjust for flavor and add the bay leaves and sambal oelek. If necessary, thicken with kuzu or arrowroot.

Eggplant sauce

4 SERVINGS

2 eggplants
1 onion
1 clove garlic
1 spoonful vegetable oil
1 cup vegetable broth
thyme

Cook the whole eggplants in an oven at 200°C for about 30 minutes, allow to cool and peel.
Sauté the onion and garlic in a little vegetable oil.
Mix the eggplant pulp, the onion and roasted garlic with a little vegetable stock and thyme until soft and creamy.
If necessary pass it through a sieve.

Black olive sauce

4 SERVINGS

100 g pitted black olives
1 spoonful miso
100 ml water
1 clove garlic
thyme

Blend all the ingredients for a few minutes.

Red turnip sauce

4 SERVINGS

juice of 3 red turnip
1 spoonful kuzu
1 teaspoonful wasabi

Simmer the red turnip juice, bind it with the kuzu previously dissolved in a little warm water for a few minutes and add the wasabi.

Celery sauce

4 SERVINGS

3 celery ribs
200 ml vegetable stock
1 spoonful arrowroot or kuzu

Cut the celery into small pieces and cook for at least 20 minutes in the vegetable stock. Blend well and thicken with kuzu or arrowroot.

Tofu sauce

4 SERVINGS

150 g of tofu
2 spoonfuls extra virgin olive oil
2 spoonfuls apple cider vinegar
2 spoonfuls mustard
1 spoonful tamari
1 small bunch of dill
parsley
vegetable broth

Blend all the ingredients for a few minutes.

Yogurt sauce

4 SERVINGS

125 g natural yoghurt
1 spoonful apple cider vinegar
2 spoonfuls extra virgin olive oil
½ teaspoonful tamari
½ spoonful mustard
herbs (thyme, tarragon, parsley, basil, coriander, chervil)

Blend all the ingredients for a few minutes.

Lime vinaigrette

4 SERVINGS

1 dl olive oil
juice of 2 limes
1 spoonful apple cider vinegar
1 spoonful mustard
1 fresh green chili julienned
½ cucumber, cut into narrow strips
sea salt

Blend all ingredients for 30 seconds.
Add the red chili and garnish with the strips of cucumber.

drinks hot and cold

Ginger energy drink

INGREDIENTS

2 untreated lemons
1 stalk lemongrass
200 g fresh ginger
1 teaspoonful agave syrup

Simmer all the ingredients in 1 liter of water for 40 minutes. Strain and add the agave syrup.

Canarino

INGREDIENTS

zest of 1 untreated lemon
1 teaspoonful agave syrup

Put the lemon zest in a tumbler, add the hot water and the agave syrup.
Serve piping hot.

Hot lemon

INGREDIENTS

1 cinnamon pod
4 untreated lemons
4 teaspoonfuls agave syrup

Simmer 1 liter of water with the cinnamon pod.
Leave in infusion for 5 minutes.
Meanwhile, squeeze the lemons and keep the juice in a container. Add the agave syrup to the water and pour in the lemon juice.
Serve piping hot.

Anti-cellulite tisane

INGREDIENTS

10 g of fucus
20 g fennel root
30 grams meadowsweet

Simmer 1 liter of water. Use 1 teaspoonful of each herb per cup. Pour into the infuser, cover with simmering water and leave to infuse for a few minutes

Fat-burning tisane

INGREDIENTS

10 g meadowsweet flowers
20 g birch leaves
30 g blackcurrant leaves

Simmer 1 liter of water. Use 1 teaspoonful of each herb per cup. Pour in the infuser, cover with simmering water and allow to infuse for a few minutes.

Circulatory tisane

INGREDIENTS

20 g of grapevine leaves
10 g of blackcurrant
10 g of verbena
lemon juice

Simmer 1 liter of water. Use 1 teaspoonful of each herb per cup. Pour into the infuser, cover with simmering water and allow to infuse for a few minutes.
Drink 2 cups a day, flavoring it with lemon juice. Use low sodium water.

Wellness tisane

INGREDIENTS

5 g burdock
5 g birch
5 g dandelion
5 g orange blossom
5 g fennel
5 g nettle
5 g licorice
5 g lime

Simmer 1 liter of water. Select 3 herbs to taste, and use 1 teaspoonful of each herb per cup. Pour into the infuser, cover with boiling water and allow to infuse for a few minutes.
Drink 2 cups, morning and evening.

Fruit water

INGREDIENTS

3 figs
3 plums
3 dried apricots
1 apple sliced
1 pear, sliced
1 untreated lemon sliced
2 spoonfuls agave syrup

Put all ingredients in 1 liter of water and bring to boiling point. Allow to infuse for 15 minutes and filter. Add a little agave syrup at the end. Drink cold.

Sassy Water

INGREDIENTS

1 cucumber
1 untreated lemon
1 handful of fresh mint leaves

Peel a small cucumber and cut into little pieces. Wash and cut a lemon into thin slices.
Pour the whole into a pitcher and add the mint leaves and 1.5 liters of water. Stir, cover and leave overnight in a cool place.

Pineapple-coconut

INGREDIENTS

20 cl pineapple juice
20 cl coconut milk
4 teaspoonfuls agave syrup
1 cup crushed ice

Combine all the ingredients in the blender for one minute. Serve cold.

Light fruit drink

INGREDIENTS

15 g orange blossom
3 spoonfuls agave syrup
4 spoonfuls lemon juice
50 cl grape juice
a few slices of untreated orange and lemon

Infuse the orange blossoms in 50 cl of piping hot water. Filter and add the agave syrup, lemon juice and grape juice.
Serve hot or cold with slices of orange and lemon.

Cool cucumber

Ingredients

2 cucumbers
2 ribs of celery
600 g apples
1 teaspoonful soy sauce
tabasco

Wash the vegetables and apples and juice them.
Add the soy sauce and a dash of tabasco.
Mix and pour into a glass with ice cubes and garnish with celery ribs.
Serve well chilled.

Vegetable Smoothie

Ingredients

2 cucumbers
400 g melon
60 cl cranberry or pomegranate juice
20 cl soy cream
a few fresh mint leaves

Clean and peel the vegetables and fruit.
Cut into cubes and place in the blender with the juice and cream. Blend for a few seconds.
Serve cold, garnished with fresh mint.

Green smoothie

Ingredients

1 cucumber
1 avocado
4 kiwis
50 cl apple juice
2 spoonfuls agave syrup

Clean and peel the vegetables and fruit.
Cut into cubes and place in the blender with the apple juice and agave syrup.
Blend for a few seconds.
Serve well chilled.

Tomato juice

INGREDIENTS

600 g tomatoes
1 teaspoonful Worcestershire sauce
tabasco
1 teaspoonful lemon juice
1 cup crushed ice
1 spoonful celery salt
2 stalks celery, cut into sticks

Wash the vegetables and juice them. Pour the juice into a shaker and mix with the other ingredients. Garnish with a piece of celery and serve well chilled.

Hibiscus flower tea

INGREDIENTS

a handful of dried hibiscus flowers
1 cinnamon pod
chopped fresh ginger
1 clove
1 piece of chili
juice of 1 orange
juice of 1 Persian lime or key lime
1 teaspoonful honey

Wash the hibiscus flowers. Put the cinnamon pod, fresh ginger and the clove in one liter of piping hot water and infuse for a few minutes.
Then add the hibiscus flowers and infuse for another 10 minutes. Add the rest of the ingredients.
Must be served chilled and can be stored for up to 4 days at a temperature of 3 °C.

Index of recipes

Sauces and dressings

Drinks hot and cold

Photo credits

Erwan Frotin: pp. 45, 46, 47, 48-49, 50-51, 63, 65, 66, 67, 70, 77, 79, 80-81, 82-83, 84-85, 90-91, 94, 95, 96-97, 105, 106-107, 116, 117, 122, 123, 124, 135.

Manuela Vanni: pp. 52-53, 54-55, 56-57, 58, 59, 61, 69, 71, 72-73, 74-75, 86-87, 88-89, 92, 93, 99, 100-101, 103, 109, 110-111, 112, 113, 115, 118-119, 120-121, 125.

Production of the English edition
Studio g.due, Milan